Nurse Autumn's Secret Love

Nurse Autumn's Secret Love

Colleen L. Reece

Thorndike Press • Chivers Press
Thorndike, Maine USA   Bath, England

This Large Print edition is published by Thorndike Press, USA
and by Chivers Press, England.

Published in 2001 in the U.S. by arrangement
with Colleen L. Reece.

Published in 2001 in the U.K. by arrangement
with the author.

U.S. Hardcover 0-7862-3137-8 (Candlelight Series Edition)
U.K. Hardcover 0-7540-4457-2 (Chivers Large Print)

The text of this Large Print edition is unabridged.
Other aspects of the book may vary from the original edition.

Set in 16 pt. Plantin by Elena Picard.

Printed in the United States on permanent paper.

British Library Cataloguing-in-Publication Data available

Library of Congress Cataloging-in-Publication Data

Reece, Colleen L.
    Nurse Autumn's secret love / Colleen L. Reece.
        p. cm.
    ISBN 0-7862-3137-8 (lg. print : hc : alk. paper)
    1. Nurses — Fiction. 2. Physicians — Fiction.
    3. Amnesia — Fiction.   4. Sisters — Fiction. 5. Twins —
Fiction. 6. Utah — Fiction. 7. Large type books.
    I. Title.
    PS3568.E3646 N85 2001
        813'.54—dc21   00-053630

Nurse Autumn's Secret Love

Chapter 1

The early morning sun was just topping the huge red-rock mountain when Autumn Dale stepped from her doorway. For a moment she hesitated, then, without thought for any possible audience, stretched her arms wide, embracing the new day.

"I'm so glad I'm alive!" Her face sobered as she remembered . . . Was it only a year since . . . but she quickly turned her thoughts away from the past. There was no use in looking back. It only brought pain and heartache. The small chin below the determined lips tilted up a fraction. This was her season, the beginning of autumn. She would rejoice, be glad, and perhaps even forget.

Autumn's steps were quick as she walked along the deserted street. It was too early in the morning for the usual small clusters of people to appear. She had planned it this way. She wanted to get to Big Rock Hospital

before the doctor. There were several patients to check on, to see how they had come
through the night. But the fresh air, the
beauty of the morning, slowed her down.

How I love this place! She felt like shouting
it to the world, awakening the neighbors,
proclaiming to them how lucky they were.
Instead, Autumn only laughed aloud. And
the sea-green eyes set in the white skin with
only a trace of freckles were at peace with
the world. The sun had selected her auburn
hair as a fitting target. Now little golden rays
shot through it. It was lovely hair, soft and
slightly curly, topped by the starched white
cap of her profession.

"Good morning, Letty!"

The gray-haired woman at the hospital
desk looked up. There was a new note in
Autumn's voice. A wave of thankfulness
went through Letty Williams. She had loved
the girl since she had assisted at her birth,
over twenty years ago. But it had been a long
time since she had heard Autumn speak like
this. Too long, far too long.

"Morning, Autumn. We had a quiet
night."

Taking the charts down, Autumn quickly
went over them. The burn case, the broken
leg, the three cases of flu, the concussion
case.

"All are well, doing fine," Letty said. "I wouldn't be surprised if most of them were dismissed today." She hesitated, then an impish smile appeared on her face. "And, oh, yes, of course . . . there's Dr. McBain."

Autumn stifled a giggle. "How is he?"

"Itching and miserable, mad at himself and everyone else." Letty dropped her brisk reporting manner entirely. "Can't blame the poor man. Comes out to take over part of the hospital duties from Dr. Archer and tangles with a patch of poison oak on his first ride out to see a patient!"

They laughed together. Dr. McBain hadn't been with them long enough to prove himself. It wasn't a very good beginning. He had been the worst patient imaginable, impatient to be up and active. Instead, he had been so thoroughly covered with the poison oak rash, Dr. Archer had ordered him to stay in the hospital until it was gone.

Letty stood up, stretching. "Well, I'd better get on home." Her eyes softened as she looked at Autumn. "Sure am glad you decided to move in with me. What with me on nights and you working days, we don't see each other much. But at least I know you're there." She stretched again. "Me, I'm headed for some lovely sleep. See you at dinner, Autumn." Her rounded frame in its neat uniform, still crisp after the night's work, disappeared out the door.

For a moment Autumn watched Letty go. They had a good setup here. Maxine Phillips was the third of the nursing staff at Big Rock. She liked working swing shift, for her husband also worked those hours. She was slight and dark, and just as efficient as Autumn or Letty. She was also invaluable when it came to making home calls. Some of Maxine's ancestors were Indians, and she had always lived in Dale. She knew every trail and crossing and canyon from Bryce to Zion to Cedar Breaks. Southern Utah was as familiar to her as the palm of her own hand. While Autumn had been born and raised in Dale, the town named after her great-grandfather, Maxine had an advantage over her because Maxine's relatives were scattered over a hundred-mile radius.

Autumn sighed. *If only all the patients would come to Big Rock Hospital instead of calling the doctors out to where they lived!* But a lot of the ranchers, sheepherders, Indians, and townspeople felt it was better to be taken care of at home. Dr. Archer had never refused to go on what the people at the hospital called "ride-out calls." But what would Dr. McBain do? Matthew McBain, M.D. Tall, hair fiery red instead of auburn like

10

Autumn's, eyes definitely green and hard as emeralds. She had gasped when she first saw him, not heeding Dr. Archer's chuckle.

"Two redheads on the staff," Dr. Archer had said. "Things should liven up around here!"

Autumn's automatic response was, "My hair's auburn, not red." And it didn't even register.

One thing about Matthew McBain, he was a man to get things done. If he set his course, the devil himself wouldn't be able to change his mind.

The persistent flashing of a call light interrupted Autumn's thoughts. She straightened, noticing it was from Dr. McBain's bed, and walked silently down the short hall on her rubber-soled shoes. Her day had begun.

"About time! What does a man have to do around here to get any attention, scream and frighten everyone else in the hospital?"

Autumn was unprepared for Dr. McBain's thrust. Angry color filled her face, but she bit her tongue, counting to ten before answering.

"I wouldn't advise screaming. Think of what it would do to the image of the brand-new doctor." She kept her tone light while poking the thermometer under his tongue, ignoring his fervent protests. "Doctor's orders." The emerald green eyes glared at her. Thank heavens they had the new type of hospital thermometers that took only seconds instead of three minutes. She couldn't have endured that stare.

"Normal."

His response could only be called a grunt. "I knew it would be. It's stupid, I tell you, just plain stupid for me to be here!" Dr. McBain pounded the bed table, making it jump. He failed to note the twinkle in Autumn's eyes or the sudden demure look that erased any trace of insubordination.

"You'd frighten the patients if you were up and around now, Doctor." She took a small mirror from the chest of drawers nearby.

He looked at her suspiciously, but could only see innocence. "I guess you're right." Some of the swelling had gone down from his face, but the eyelids were still partially closed. He lay back, defeated. Curiously enough the simple action got through to Autumn.

"I'm sorry this all happened, Doctor. By tomorrow it should be almost gone." Her tone was gentle, the kindest he had heard since meeting her.

His lips opened to ask a question, but with

a smile she was gone. There were sounds of stirring from the other patients. She had no time now to chat. But as he heard her moving from room to room, her voice carried. She had left the door open — purposely? The walls were adobe and muffled sounds. But with the door open he could hear her, especially when she was in the room directly across from his own. His eyebrows registered approval of the low, friendly voice. She talked with each patient as she worked, answering questions, encouraging them. She would be a good one to have on his staff.

His staff. He smiled wryly. Everyone at medical school and later the hospital where he had interned, then served as resident, had thought he would snatch a plum, a big, busy hospital. He had thought so, too. Then shortly before he had to decide between two big hospitals, his old friend, Dr. Archer, had visited him.

"How would you like to take over a small hospital, twelve beds, most of them empty most of the time? I can't offer you a high salary." He named a figure, ridiculous when compared to Dr. McBain's other two offers. "You'll be run ragged with ride-out calls, and —"

"What's a ride-out call?"

13

"A lot of the people won't come in to the hospital so we ride out to where they live. Sometimes by jeep, once in a while, even by horseback."

Matthew McBain threw his head back and laughed. "Hard work. Low salary. Partially empty hospital. What can you offer on the plus side?"

Dr. Archer wasn't daunted. He had known Matt since childhood. He knew that beneath the fiery thatch there was a cool, calculating brain. But he also knew there were ideals and a very big heart.

"I can offer you the knowledge that you're doing a good job. I can offer you three nurses who can't be beat. I can offer you the able — if slowing down — assistance of yours truly, Dr. Archer."

The younger doctor stared. There was something in his friend's voice that prevented him from just laughing and telling him no on the spot.

"Tell me about this . . . this Paradise." His tone was mocking, but his eyes were interested.

Dr. Archer smiled. He had hooked Matt's interest. Now to land him! "Dale, Utah. Not far from Bryce, Zion, and Cedar Breaks Canyons. Red-rock country, beautiful beyond belief! Spicy cedar and hot blue skies. A land of contrasts. A hard land, for those who live there. We aren't too far from Kanab. They make a lot of movies just out of there. Sometimes we get patients from them.

"The town was named for Jedediah Dale, a pioneer. He saw richness in the red dirt and was one of the first men to use irrigation. He had the money behind him, and he used it well. It turned Dale into a garden spot. You should see the green vegetation of the town. Why, Matt, it's an oasis! He had deep, deep wells dug. He traced and found springs. None of this desert alkali water for Dale! It's pure and sweet, and cold enough to chill your teeth. People came, and saw, and stayed."

Matt looked at him keenly. "And you were one of them."

"Yes. When I saw that peaceful little town by the big red-rock mountain, I felt as if I'd come home." Abruptly his voice changed. "There's one thing I have to warn you about." He could see the cynical look on Matt's face, as if Matt expected to hear of a big catch. Dr. Archer leaned forward. "I went there for a while. I hadn't really set a time limit for myself. But it was only supposed to be a short while. And I've been there over thirty years."

"That long!" Matt had known but had

forgotten to keep track. He himself was almost thirty and Dr. Archer had lived in Dale ever since he could remember. Even when Matt had been a child in Salt Lake City, the doctor had visited them from Dale now and then. There had been a wife then. There had also been a dad and mom for Matt, but they were all gone now, leaving him and Dr. Archer to carry on alone.

"You mentioned three nurses. Who are they?"

Dr. Archer hid his smile and kept his voice casual. "First comes Letty Williams, God bless her! She's about my age, gray-haired, kind, and a dandy nurse. She's lived in Dale a long time. In fact, she came at my request when I decided to stay. Everyone knows and likes her, even if her tongue is sharp. She minces no words, that's for sure."

Matt wondered if Dr. Archer had lost some rounds with his highly efficient nurse!

"Then there's Maxine Phillips. She's part Indian and knows the country. You'll like her. She's calm, topnotch. I use her in surgery an awful lot." He hesitated.

Matt sensed he was having difficulty. "And the third nurse?"

"Autumn Dale."

"Autumn Dale! What kind of a name is that?"

Dr. Archer just looked at him. "It's what her grandfather wanted her named. She was born in late September, the time of year he loved. But he wasn't there to see it. The spring before he had had some heart problems. I told him he'd have to slow down. He wouldn't. I think at the last he knew he wasn't going to make it. Just a few days before he died he told his son, 'If it's a girl, will you name her Autumn?' He died just a month before she was born."

Dr. Archer sighed, looking out the window, but not seeing the tall buildings in the distance. In another moment he was laughing again. "The old rascal! That was Ephraim, Jedediah's son. And he knew I was hampered by only having a small clinic to work from. So in his will he made a provision for a small but perfectly equipped hospital for Dale. He had talked it over with his son and daughter-in-law, Autumn's parents. They agreed. They were the unselfish kind of people who would rather that the town had a hospital than live in luxury themselves."

"Were?"

A shade crossed the old doctor's face. "Yes. They were killed in a plane crash last spring." He started to add something else, then held it back.

17

Matt could sense the struggle but didn't urge him. If it were something he should know, Dr. Archer would tell him. But the moments lengthened until Matt asked, "Then this granddaughter, this Autumn Dale, is your third nurse?"

There was no hesitance in Dr. Archer now. His face positively glowed. "Is she ever! While the townspeople like Letty and Maxine, they love Autumn. Not for her grandfather's sake, or her great-grandfather's sake, either, but for her own. She is as concerned about the smallest child, the poorest family, as the town banker. She has a simple, natural caring. And her looks! I can't call her beautiful. She's more than that. She has auburn hair. Her eyes look like the sea, always changing. She even has a few freckles. She's tall and slim and —"

"Hold it!" Matt said. "You'll overwhelm me before I even see her!"

Matthew McBain made a sour face. "You should have been a salesman. Yes, I'll come. But I won't promise how long I'll stay."

Matt's telephone rang as Dr. Archer gripped his hand across the desk. Matt turned toward it, waving, as his older friend went out the door.

But he didn't hear Dr. Archer's low-growled comment to himself. "You'll stay, my friend. I can count on the beauties of Dale to see to that." The doctor chuckled and swung down the stairs, scorning the elevator filled with lazy bodies. No one heard his added remark, or would have understood if they had. "Ah, yes, perhaps even the beauties of Autumn Dale!"

Back upstairs Dr. Matthew McBain had finished his call and stamped to the window. As Dr. Archer had done earlier, now Matt stood staring out the window, not seeing the tall buildings. He was seeing a mentally inspired vision of a little town, a huge red-rock mountain, a small hospital built of adobe and painted white, surrounded by green vegetation.

"An oasis in the desert," Dr. Archer had described it. Would Dale live up to its preview? Strange that in all the years they had known each other, Matt had never been there. Too busy, he thought, just plain too busy. Now what had he let himself in for? Starting his career in some obscure corner of the world where one accepted custom of caring for patients was riding out to where they were!

He shuddered. There would be some changes made, he could tell them that! They could learn that the hospital was the best place to get well, and they could learn it in one big hurry.

Now several weeks later, restlessly stirring in one of the beds of that same hospital, Dr. Matthew McBain had even more reason to feel that way, while recovering from poison oak from his very first ride-out call! And yet, he had to admit to himself, it wasn't totally unpleasant lying in bed listening to Autumn Dale's voice across the hall as she prodded, encouraged, and directed her patients. No, it wasn't unpleasant at all.

Chapter 2

Letty had been right. All six patients were released by the end of the day.

"They're well enough to go home and will actually heal faster there, especially the broken leg," Dr. Archer said. "Tommy misses his folks so much all he does is mope." The doctor firmly believed in hospitalizing patients only as long as absolutely necessary. No running up of hospital bills for unnecessary days there.

Dr. McBain was also doing well. The next day the swelling was gone, the rash nearly so. For the first time Autumn saw him really smile, glad to be free of the itching and misery. But by the end of the day she firmly wished he was back in that hospital bed! He had run her ragged.

Dr. Archer had gone on a ride-out call, leaving his day nurse to show the new man around. Dr. McBain had approved of the sparkling white rooms, the cheerful Indian-patterned curtains, and the equipment. Dr. Archer had been right. It was a perfect little hospital.

But when they came to the duty sheets, he threw up his hands in horror. "When do you nurses have time off?"

Autumn looked at him in surprise. "Why, when the patient load is down."

"What?" It was just short of a roar. His eyebrows almost met his fiery hair. "You mean to tell me you don't have regular days off?"

Autumn only laughed. "We don't have patients on a regular basis. How can we have regularly scheduled days off?" Seeing his amazement she went on. "Sometimes we will only have two or three patients in the hospital for a week. Then we trade around and take longer shifts so someone is here — and someone is free for a day. Once in a while we don't have anyone in. Then we can all be off at the same time, but on call. Then if we have several patients, we all take our regular shifts."

Dr. McBain glowered. "That's no way to run a hospital! You girls need time off on a planned basis."

"Why? We can garden or shop on Thursday as well as Monday."

"Of all the weird arrangements I have ever

heard, this is the worst! Isn't there money to hire another nurse, at least part-time?"

Autumn fought down an anger to match his own. "There's plenty. My grandfather's will carried with it enough to make up salaries when the patient load was down. It isn't money, it's unavailability. There isn't another nurse in Dale who wants to work. Most of them are busy with their families. We have three LPNs who come in on call if we have emergencies. A few months ago, the summer flu filled every bed. Those women were priceless. But most of the time we can get along on our own."

She wasn't aware of the dangerous glint that had come to her eyes, or the tilt to her chin. She was unconsciously fighting for her hospital against any criticism.

"Well! We'll have to do something about that!"

Autumn could see Dr. McBain had good intentions and softened. "If you could come up with someone who'd be willing to work part-time it would be great! Especially an LPN. But we just can't get anyone to come here on that basis regularly. I know Dr. Archer tried, but what nurse only wants a part-time job in a little town? Not many."

Matthew McBain drummed his fingers against the desk. In the back of his mind something was knocking, a faint remembrance of someone — he couldn't get it to come clear, yet he knew it was important. Brushing it aside until he could give it his full concentration, he looked at the nurse.

"Fine. I'll see what I can do." He hesitated for a moment. "You said nurses didn't want to come to a small town. How about you? Surely, you've had offers from city hospitals. Why stay here?"

She didn't see the genuine curiosity in his question, but took it as a slam. "It's my home."

He ignored the coolness and probed further. "Your parents are dead. Plane crash, wasn't it?"

"Yes."

It was several moments before he realized Autumn wasn't going to elaborate. When he did, it was with the feeling he had gone too far. To cover his embarrassment he stood.

"I think that's all for now, Nurse Dale. I'll call if I need you." It was a dismissal, short and to the point.

Autumn hid a smile. "Thank you, Dr. McBain." In a moment she was gone, leaving him staring at the door.

Have I seen her before? he wondered. *Somehow she looks familiar. Someone else who looks like her? No, but somewhere . . .*

the intercom interrupted him.

"Dr. McBain, will you come to the surgical area, please." There was nothing in the low-pitched voice to alarm the patient, who must be with Autumn, but Dr. McBain knew the nurse meant *now*. It was only a few quick strides to the small surgery. One of the blessings of a small hospital, he thought with a little smile. Pushing open the door, he saw Autumn applying direct pressure to a nasty cut on a man's arm.

"Hold it tight," the doctor ordered, stopping to wash and don gloves. "I'm going to have to make stitches." Already the merciful little vessel of local anesthetic was giving temporary relief, and by the time Dr. McBain had cleansed the wound, the stitches went in without pain.

Now he smiled at the dark-eyed man opposite him. "That should fix you up. How'd you do it?"

The man grimaced. "You won't believe it! I was cutting wood and the axe slipped."

"I'll want to see you again tomorrow. I'm sure everything will be fine, but . . ." He reached for a syringe. "I'll give you a tetanus shot just in case. Never know what germ might be on that axe blade."

Autumn spoke for the first time. "Not on Sancho's axe blade! He keeps his tools as clean as Maxine keeps her house." So this was Maxine's husband. A strong, clean-cut man. He gave Sancho the tetanus shot anyway.

"Thanks a lot, Doc," Sancho said before leaving. "Don't forget to send me a bill."

"I'll do that." Dr. McBain watched Sancho go out. "I like him. Are there many in your town like this one?"

Autumn's eyes glowed. "Many, many. He is typical of the men of Dale. We're pretty proud of them." She wouldn't have had to add her last sentence. Her pride shone in every word.

He watched her putting the little surgery back to rights. "When we get an LPN, she can do some of this for you."

Autumn shot him a funny look but didn't respond. In another minute he had gone back to the office. He wanted to familiarize himself with as many patient charts as he could. The more he knew of his new patients, the better. He had a feeling the encounter with Sancho had gone well, that his first "surgery" in Dale would be successful not only in healing but in public relations.

Matt McBain was right. In the days following, nearly every patient who came in referred to the "nice job you did on Sancho." Still, it was taking the new doctor time to

26

get used to the small-town phenomenon of everyone knowing about everyone else. But in other ways he was adjusting to life in Dale quickly. He had accepted Dr. Archer's insistent invitation and was sharing quarters with the older man.

"I'm glad you accepted," said Autumn, who was taking a break from her endless setting up of charts and supplies one afternoon. "He's been terribly lonely since he lost his wife. I had hoped someday he and Letty might —" She was stopped short by Dr. McBain's emerald stare.

"Matchmaking in addition to all your other duties, Nurse Dale? My goodness, but you're talented!"

The sarcasm brought color to her face, as it always did. How could this man, so gentle with patients, have the power to infuriate her so easily?

"Not matchmaking. But they would be happier together."

"And how about Nurse Autumn Dale? Does she have any immediate matrimonial plans?"

She couldn't know that for one instant the man within the doctor held his breath waiting for her answer. Her eyes grew glazed. "No matrimonial plans, Dr. McBain."

It wasn't until after she had gone that Matthew realized she hadn't responded to the word "immediate." She had said, "No matrimonial plans." It stirred his curiosity to an unbelievable degree. Was there some lost love in her life? He almost laughed out loud at the idea. She was only twenty-one! Not much time for having a buried love.

But he also remembered how she had explained when he asked how she could have finished training so young: "I started school when I was five, because of my birthday being at the end of September. I skipped fifth grade and graduated when I was sixteen. Even though I couldn't actually take my training until I was eighteen, because of my high grades the nursing school let me do my book work early." There was no bragging in her voice, just telling the facts, but the new doctor's respect had gone up considerably.

She was quite a girl, this Autumn Dale. Or was she more woman than girl? He had seen her comfort a child with the wisdom of a grandmother. On the other hand, he had caught her eating a drippy popsicle with all the enthusiasm of a ten-year-old.

If Dr. Matthew McBain had realized how much of his free time was being spent considering a certain nurse named Autumn

Dale, he might have been surprised at himself. He had avoided girls and women during training simply because of lack of funds. He had had little time and no money to spend on them. Now, exposed in an informal, friendly atmosphere, to this unspoiled girl-woman, his reactions were very typically male.

For a moment he considered asking Dr. Archer about Autumn's past love life but decided against it. It might create the wrong impression. He stood and stretched, then noticed the mail had been delivered. Everything was quiet; now would be a good time to get it out of the way.

It was a good thing the hospital had discharged its last patient just an hour before. When Dr. McBain opened the last letter in the stack, he let out a war whoop that could have been heard from the surgical area to the so-called maternity ward, a two-bed, enclosed room far from the other rooms. It served to bring Autumn to the door.

"Is something wrong, Dr. McBain?" She was one surprised nurse when he leaped from his chair, caught her around the waist, and laughingly waltzed her across the room. It was so out of character!

What on earth had happened to set him off like that? Autumn fought back the impulse to stay in those strong arms, and with an effort freed herself.

"Dr. McBain!" He only laughed harder, waving the letter in the air. Autumn had seen the stack of mail that came, noting the violet-scented one with the typed address. At the time she had smiled scornfully. So he was like all the rest. Women after him, probably spoiling him. Now her heart sank. She wouldn't admit even to herself she had hoped he would be a little different. Why should it matter? *She* certainly wasn't interested in him, was she? Not except as a good doctor, she told herself furiously. Never anything but that. But a perverse little echo whispered in her ear, *Oh, yeah?* She ignored it and turned back.

"She's coming!" he exclaimed.

"Who's coming?"

"Our new part-time LPN."

Autumn was speechless. It had been days and days since their little talk. If she had thought of it at all, she would have thought Dr. McBain had forgotten all about it. Now this.

"Sit down, will you, Autumn?"

Part of her churned-up mind noted the use of her first name, for the first time since he had arrived. Again her lip curled. Love did strange things to people, didn't it! She'd be willing to bet he was so excited over this girl or woman who had written to him he never even knew he had called her Autumn! He failed to see the disdainful look in her eyes as he spoke.

"You'll really like her. She's just what we need down here."

Oh, she is, is she? Autumn's mind was running on a double track. While part of it listened to Dr. McBain, the other part was saying, *We got along perfectly all right before you sent for her. In fact, even before you came. Why, of a sudden, is it so wonderful for this part-time LPN, who I'm supposed to really like to be coming?*

Dr. McBain was too happy to even notice the high color in his nurse's face. "She's such a gentle person, and she's been through so much."

Suddenly his words got through to Autumn. She leaned forward, intent on his story.

"Several months ago I was called in to observe and work with an unusual case. A young woman, scarcely more than a girl, had been picked up on the street near the hospital, wandering around. She had no purse, no identifying marks of any kind. When we got her in the hospital, she collapsed. We found a large lump on her head.

31

Somehow she must have fallen, or even been struck."

Autumn's mouth softened in sympathy.

"When she awoke, she was terrified — she could remember nothing. Nothing! Not her name, not any other name that might help. She was wearing a plain skirt and sweater that couldn't be traced to any particular store. Without money, or friends, it was a big, lonely world for her. When she was better, I asked the hospital head if we couldn't find her something to do.

"It was as if she had been born, a full-grown person, in that hospital bed the morning she woke. She had no trouble eating, dressing, or with personal care. But she had no memory of her former life at all. The more I saw her, the more I felt she had what is sometimes called a traumatic shock. She wasn't remembering because she didn't want to remember. There was far more to her memory loss than just falling or being hit; something pretty terrible must have happened to her to keep her from remembering.

"We all helped as much as we could. At first she worked as an aide. Then we saw she had had some training of some kind. She was a natural-born nurse. This gave us a few clues and we contacted all the hospitals around, but they didn't have any missing nurses."

He broke off sharply. "Autumn, what is it?"

Her face had gone paper-white, the color of her uniform. "No . . . no, it couldn't be!"

"Couldn't be what?"

She shook her head, trying desperately to control herself. "My twin sister."

If the heavens had opened at that moment and an angel had appeared, Matt McBain couldn't have been more surprised. "Twin sister?" He was thunderstruck. No one had mentioned a twin sister. Yet there had been that strange hesitancy on Dr. Archer's part when they had been discussing Autumn.

Autumn moistened her dry lips, forcing the words out. "Yes. I had a twin sister, but not identical. We don't really look alike, or didn't."

"Didn't?"

There was anguish in the nurse's eyes. "I don't know if she's still living."

"What a strange thing to say! Do you want to tell me about it?" For a long time he didn't think she would answer.

When she did, it was with all the fire of a zombie, forcing each word out painfully. "Even though we didn't look alike, we were closer than many identical twins. We did everything together, shared the same ideas, ideals, and went into nurses' training together. It was all planned. We'd come back to Dale and work together in Big Rock Hospital. Then it happened. She fell in love. He was worthless, a drifter. All she saw was the romance, the glamour of being in love. What she didn't know was that any girl was easy game to him, or so he thought."

Her voice grew lower. "She came home one night our last month in training. He was there, but he had decided a sister might do as well for his cheap tricks. She came in as I was shoving him away, calling him everything I could think of. All her feelings died for him. She ordered him out.

"I didn't think she'd make it through the rest of training, but she did. When it came time for us to come back to Dale, she left a note and simply disappeared. She said she needed time to be alone. Please, would we not try and find her. It almost broke Dad and Mom's heart. For a while we did as she asked. Then it was too much. Someone said they'd seen her in Salt Lake City, and the folks went to Kanab and caught a plane there. The plane crashed coming into the Salt Lake City airport."

A great wave of sympathy for this valiant girl before him filled Matt. He could barely restrain the urge to hold her close and tell her he would protect her from any more pain. Yet so intent was he on her story his own unpredictable feelings took second place.

"That could explain it. If she really was in Salt Lake City she would have read about the crash — and the list of passengers. Maybe she started out to find them, you know, looking in hospitals. If she fell, or was struck, when she came to, it was with her mind refusing to accept it all. Maybe she even felt intuitively they were coming for her, and blamed herself for their death."

"You really think this girl may be my sister, don't you?" The agony in the whisper reached him.

Dr. McBain paused, unwilling to give her false hope. "What was — is her name?"

"April. They named us April and Autumn."

Matthew McBain's desk chair crashed unheeded to the floor and he stood, eyes burning green.

"The girl in the hospital . . . the amnesiac . . . we tried all kinds of names on her. But when she asked what month it was, and we told her April, for the first time her eyes lit up. Because of that, we decided to call her April!"

Chapter 3

For a moment Dr. McBain thought Autumn would pass out. Her face turned dead-white. But only for a moment. With a visible effort she controlled her shaking hands, and a glorious flag of red color stained her face.

"April!" It was a cry from her depths. Its appeal was too much for even rock-ribbed Matthew McBain. In one stride he was at her side, holding her in strong arms. She resisted only momentarily. Then with a little sigh she hid her face in his white jacket and sobbed out all the misery she had been carrying inside since April's disappearance and the death of her parents.

From her position she could not see his face. She could not see the conflicting emotions as he looked down at the bent head and tightened his grip on her. But for the man who had avoided women so long, she was a revelation, this slim girl in his arms. She was so warm, so appealing, so almost helpless standing there, sobbing in his arms. He sensed this was not usual for her, the giving way of a dam inside that held her emotions in check. These moments were more precious to him because of their rarity. Matthew McBain set his jaw grimly. So this was it. Love. After all his scorching remarks, his scoffing at those who proclaimed "love at first sight," an auburn-haired girl from a little town in Utah had done what others failed to do.

A great wave of longing swept through him. He could almost understand the primitive feelings of cavemen who caught their women and took them to a secluded cave away from any other man. He was horrified to feel a great peal of laughter at the thought starting deep inside. If he laughed now, it would be disastrous. Instead, he tightened his hold until she could feel the thumping of his heart.

Was it a minute, ten, or an hour that they stood there, each lost in emotion? For Autumn it was release, for Matthew it was recognition. He had discovered one of the elemental secrets of creation, the love of a strong man for a woman. But he knew this was no time to proclaim himself. He could take advantage of her emotion, lean down and kiss her. She might even respond. Rich color went through his face and he jerked his head back from temptation.

No, when he kissed Autumn Dale, it would be under different circumstances, not when she was unstrung and had her defenses down. But the time would come when he would kiss her and offer himself. What a life they could make! He closed his eyes, thinking of his parents whose thirty-eight years together had been a daily revelation of love and understanding. That's the way it would be with Autumn. No passing fancy, no trip to the altar with a marriage license in one hand, divorce papers in the other. She would be steady, constant, and gloriously true to her man.

The thought caused Matt to loosen his hold, to tenderly lift his big surgeon's hand and smooth the auburn waves back from her tear-stained face. It was his touch that brought Autumn back to the present. She had not been thinking of him as anything except a port in a storm, someone who could understand what she'd been through. But his hand gently touching her hair made her self-conscious.

"Oh!" she said, pulling away, her own hands going to her disheveled hair, her face red as fire. For just one moment she wondered at the look in his eyes, a look of kindness, tenderness . . . and something more. Something she refused to consider at that time.

In her nervousness she blurted out the first thing she thought of. "Oh, Dr. McBain, I've drowned you!"

It was the touch needed to release Matt from his self-imposed silence. He had gone from disbelief to attraction to acceptance to forcing himself to remain calm in just those few moments. Now he laughed, from the toes up. Great shouts of laughter, irresistible to Autumn. She joined him. It was fortunate Big Rock Hospital was having an off day. Any patient would have thought they were crazy.

When they finally settled down and were a safe distance apart, Matt leaned his arms on the desk.

"We have to decide what's best to do."

"Best to do?" Autumn looked at him inquiringly. "Why, I'll go right to Salt Lake City, and . . ."

He was shaking his head. "No, Autumn." He could see flags of disagreement waving in her eyes. Patiently he explained, knowing her own training with nursing would help her understand.

"When April — if this girl is April — remembers all the things that led to her winding up in the hospital, she's going to have a lot to face. The death of your parents. The loss of faith in one she loved. It's a big load, Autumn."

She could see that, and leaned back in her chair.

"I think it would be best to go ahead with our original plans. Bring her down here. Put her to work. It's a familiar setting, she will remember . . . in time. But don't rush her."

"How can I see her, my own sister, and not tell her who she is?" There was despair in Autumn's voice, and yet she knew he was right. To rush April back to reality might be the worst thing in the world for her.

"You live with Letty Williams, don't you?"

Autumn nodded.

"Do you still own your old home, the one your grandfather built?"

Again Autumn nodded; this time her breath quickened. He had something in mind, that was obvious. But when it came it surprised her.

"Do you suppose Letty would close her house for a while, or even consider renting it out, say, for a few months?"

"Why, I don't know. I suppose so, if there were a reason."

His eyes were steady. "There is a reason, a

good reason. I want you to reopen your old home and move back there. I'll tell April, or the girl we called April, I've found a place for her to stay. She mentioned it in her letter. The normal surroundings, coupled with a lot of patience, will do more to bring her back than anything I know. She'll be right there, among familiar things, perhaps even in her own room."

There was gratitude in Autumn's eyes. Wordlessly she reached her hand across the desk to Matt. He took it, conscious of his own racing pulse. At least she trusted him, that was a good start. Now if only he could build on that foundation.

"Why don't you go see Letty right away? Tell her what we suspect, that we may have found April, and ask if she's willing." A frown crossed his face. "Autumn?"

She was too absorbed in her own planning to notice the doubt in his voice, but his next words struck to her heart.

"Suppose it isn't your April? What then? She's still a girl, a young woman who needs love and help. Would you be willing to go ahead as planned, live in your old home with Letty and her, see if we can bring her back to the world of sunshine, away from her shadows?"

Autumn closed her eyes and swallowed

41

convulsively. She felt as if she had been hit and hit hard. Suppose it wasn't April, her twin? Could she do it? Could she accept this other girl or young woman and do everything for her she would have done for April? Suddenly she knew the answer. It had been ingrained in her since childhood. "Do unto others . . ." The Golden Rule.

"I would be proud to help her, no matter who she is."

If Dr. Matt McBain hadn't already fallen in love with Autumn, at that statement he would have tumbled irretrievably. He had watched her face her own doubt, the possibility of disappointment . . . and win. What a woman! Someday — he firmly pushed the thought aside. There was a lot to happen before that someday would arrive.

"Good." He stood up, deliberately making his voice hearty. "Go see Letty. You also might want to stop by and see Maxine Phillips and Sancho. Tell them the truth, but warn them not to spread it around." Again his brows drew together, anticipating problems before they arose, trying to smooth the way for the new LPN. "What about the townspeople? Won't they all know her?"

Autumn shook her head. "I don't know if many of them will. After the shock of her fiance's betrayal, she lost pounds and pounds. She was almost skin and bones the end of training, the last we saw her. Also, when our friend reported seeing her in Salt Lake, she said she hadn't been sure it was April. The girl she saw had blonde hair, but April's hair was soft brown, with only a hint of auburn." She broke off and looked at Matt. "What — what color hair did the girl in the hospital have?"

Matt squinted his eyes, remembering. "I don't think I ever saw her hair."

Autumn's sea-green eyes opened wide in surprise.

"They had cut it pretty short because of the head wound. When I first saw her, her head was bandaged. Later, when she worked around the hospital, she must have worn a wig. She would have had to, because her hair would have been growing out." There was pity in his glance. It was one more clue leading nowhere.

"Well, we will soon find out. If I tell her to come in two weeks, will that give you and Letty enough time to get your house opened up?"

"Of course! It never was really closed, you know. It's just that when the folks were killed six months ago, I couldn't face staying there alone. But I've still gone over every so

43

often and checked it. All it really needs is a thorough cleaning." She started for the door, then turned back.

"Dr. McBain, you'll never know how I appreciate what you're doing." She hesitated, and soft color again flooded the white skin. "And — and for providing me a place to cry."

She was gone before he could respond. It was probably just as well. Matt's iron control was slipping, and it mustn't. To her he was just Dr. McBain, a man she had worked with a few weeks, someone who had been there when she needed him. She had no way of knowing that in those minutes she had become everything in the world to him.

Someday . . . with a smile he turned back to his records. The one thing in his favor was time. In the meantime, there were charts to learn, patients to see, and some more ride-out calls to make. He groaned, thinking of his first one.

That's what came of following Dr. Archer to the wilds of southern Utah, to the canyon country. On the other hand, suppose he hadn't come? He would never have met Autumn Dale. He would not have been instrumental in restoring her twin, if April indeed proved to be her twin. Strange, the crossroads and paths men choose, and the unexpected results. With another smile, this time

44

the doctor set his mind to his work and was lost in his charts.

In Letty Williams's living room a white whirlwind had taken over. Autumn had run all the way to the cottage, bursting with her news. She was breathless when she got there, not only from the exercise in the warm October sunshine, but from the news itself.

"Letty!" Her voice preceded her into the old-fashioned kitchen where Letty was frosting a chocolate cake. She had heard Dr. Archer say how much he liked chocolate cake and had decided to make one. Now the spatula stopped in midair. What on earth was Autumn doing home at this time of day? And with that particular tone in her voice, as if someone had handed her a handful of stars on a platter!

"In here." The next moment she was encased in a hug, frosting flying. "What on earth . . ." She never finished the sentence.

"It's April, we may have found her."

The sticky spatula cascaded to the floor in its fountain of forgotten chocolate. "Found April?"

"Yes! Dr. McBain thinks she may be working in a Salt Lake City hospital right now. And, Letty, she's going to be our new LPN!"

45

It was more than the good woman could grasp. She knew that Autumn's grief had not only been for the loss of parents, but especially for April. Not knowing where she was. Hoping she was all right, yet wondering why she hadn't come for the funeral if she were alive and anywhere in the area.

"He really thinks it may be her?"

Autumn's answer was honest. "He doesn't know. But a lot of things fit. She was brought in the hospital without identification just about the time of the plane crash. She's apparently about the same age. She didn't respond to any name they tried. Finally, she asked someone what month it was. When they told her it was April, her eyes lit up, so they called her that."

Letty looked at Autumn soberly. "It isn't a whole lot to go on, Autumn. You know that. What if she isn't your twin?"

But Autumn had already fought that battle. "Then I'll help her with everything in me to find out who she really is . . . and hope that somewhere, someone is doing the same for my sister."

Letty could feel her eyes stinging with tears.

"Letty, I need your help." Quickly she sketched in Dr. McBain's plan, to reopen the house, to live there, to have the new LPN with them.

"Will you do it?"

For a moment Letty looked around her cozy kitchen, the white curtains at the windows. She loved her own little house, and yet . . . "Of course I'll do it. Ever know me not to help you out when you were in a scrape?" The sharp comment was belied by the gentleness in her eyes.

But Autumn laughed. "You'll have to admit there were a lot of scrapes, too! Remember when I fell from the roof after we'd gone to the circus and I decided I wanted to be a tightrope walker?"

"Like to have killed yourself that time!" Letty's reminder was grim, but Autumn wasn't in a grim mood.

"We have a lot to do. She's coming in two weeks."

"Two weeks!" Letty threw her hands in the air. "It will take two weeks to get that house cleaned!"

Autumn knew it was her way of accepting the challenge. "I have to stop by and see Maxine." Her hand on the door, she hesitated. "Suppose it isn't April and she doesn't like us?"

"Of all the things to think of! Get out of here and let me clean up this mess. Of

47

course she'll like us. We're nice people, aren't we?" Letty brandished the smeary spatula until Autumn disappeared. But when she was gone, Letty dropped into a chair, a little prayer rising inside her.

"Please, let it be our April. We need her." In another moment she was on her hands and knees snorting over the messy floor, already thinking ahead to the best place to start cleaning the old Dale place.

There was no lack of room. Besides Autumn's and April's rooms, there were several other bedrooms. No one would feel crowded or pressured. Letty nodded wisely. Dr. McBain was a smart one. Any girl who was fighting her way back to reality would need space to be alone when she chose and the presence of others in the house when she needed them. Her heart went out to the girl, whoever she might be. Then and there an unknown girl named April for want of a better name gained a friend, sight unseen.

Maxine and Sancho Phillips's reaction was the same as Letty's.

"How wonderful!" Maxine's dark face glowed. "Not only can we use her, but I know we can help her. Especially if she's our April."

Autumn appreciated her use of the pronoun "our." It made her feel everyone was on her side. "Even if she isn't, we'll help her." Her conviction was staunch.

Sancho laughed. "With you two and Letty Williams around, she'll get well in spite of herself." His dark eyes flashed, his white teeth shone. He was proud of his Maxine and he thought the world of Autumn and Letty.

"You'll have her taking the ride-out calls pretty soon, and both get fat and lazy while she does all the work." He ducked the pillow Maxine hurled at his head and fired one parting shot. "Now to make it all perfect, if you can just arrange for our new doc to fall in love with her, you'll have yourself a cozy little game going. Doctor's wife, LPN, or if she's April she's an RN. Yup, that would be just perfect."

He didn't notice Autumn's sea-green eyes open wide, or the way she swallowed hard. She'd never thought of that aspect of it. Now that it had been brought up, she wasn't sure if she liked it. Maxine caught the stricken look but wisely ignored it. If Autumn had begun to like the new doctor, it was her business, not theirs.

"Why don't I bring the curtains over here and wash them? You and Letty will have plenty to do cleaning." Her commonplace planning snapped Autumn to attention,

49

forcing other thoughts away.

"Great. That will really help."

They planned for a few more minutes, then Autumn rose.

"I should get back to the hospital. Just because Dr. McBain gave me time off, he didn't say I had the rest of the day." She waved back from the gate to Maxine in the doorway.

But Maxine's eyes were serious. The slump in Autumn's shoulders as she walked back to the hospital had not been there when she came. Had Autumn finally been bitten by the love bug she had swatted away so long? Maxine thought of the doctor. Craggy, emerald green eyes, very masculine, fiery red hair and temper to match.

"He's attractive, all right. Attractive enough to attract almost any woman." Then, almost under her breath, she said, "But I'm glad I've got my Sancho. I wouldn't trade him for any red-headed doctor in the world!" With a flip of her apron she slipped back into the house, smiling at her own nonsense, her heart lifting with pride even after all these years of marriage. Yes, Sancho was her life, and because of it, she was a blessed and happy woman.

Chapter 4

The tiny room was empty except for the bed where April would sleep tonight, this last night in Salt Lake City. Her few clothes, mostly uniforms contributed by the kind nurses at the hospital, were packed in luggage given her as a going-away gift. In the closet hung the beautiful blue suit, a gift from the supervisor of nurses.

"You'll need one good suit to arrive in," she had told April. "Your skirt and sweater will be fine for time off, until after your first payday. And on duty, you'll wear uniforms most of the time." She didn't add that Dr. McBain had sent the money for the suit. She had wondered at the time, but then, he was known for his kindness.

She also had no way of knowing it had been Autumn who thoughtfully handed the doctor a check, saying, "Somehow she needs to know she has something of her own. I know how I'd feel in such a case." She didn't add April would want to look nice for the doctor after all he had done for her. But she had known she would, wondering at the pang that went through her at the thought.

Now April's new suit was waiting. But it was not of clothes or even of tomorrow the girl was thinking. She was standing in front of the wall mirror, clenching white fingers, staring into her own blue eyes, eyes that were filled with stark terror.

Somewhere in the hall a board creaked. With a gasp the frozen girl rushed to the door, turning the key. Why, she did not know. But as she felt the knob slowly turn under her hand, she held her breath. For a long time she stood there, unable to move. Then the knob slid gently back in place, another board creaked, and furtive steps moved away from her door.

Taking care to turn off the light behind her so she would not be targeted against its glare, April slipped to the window, raised the curtain a few inches, and waited. Yes, he was there again, that figure in the dark coat. There was just enough light from the corner streetlight to show it was the same man. He had sneaked — there was no other word for it — from the side entrance of her hotel.

Now he stood looking up at April's window. Thank God she had turned out the light. What if she hadn't locked the door at the exact moment she had? Would he have come into her room, forced his way in, demanding . . . but there her mind went blank. Who was he? What did he want of her? Was he someone from her past? She sank to the bed, remembering the first day she had seen him.

"April, would you answer that call bell and see what the patient wants?" The floor supervisor was a good woman, but hurried. She was also a good judge of human nature. So no one knew exactly how much training April had. She was willing, obedient, and even skilled in the duties she was given. More and more the floor supervisor had allowed her to move beyond the routine jobs. Not to the point of giving medications, of course, or anything like that. But April did exactly as she was told, a rare thing in someone her age, the supervisor thought sourly. Not like some of these little flibberti-gibbets who thought they knew everything.

"See what he wants now. Heaven knows he's been demanding special service ever since he came in! You'd think he was in a private ward built for one." But her words were lost as April hurried to answer the call.

April's face was bright. It was the day she received the letter from Matthew McBain, the letter asking if she would like to come work with him in a little town called Dale, Utah, in the southern part of the state. Would she! She thought of the fiery red hair, the green eyes, the way he had fit her into the hospital. She would do anything for the big gruff doctor, anything! Hers was not a love for a man, but a hero worship for a doctor who had brought her back . . . from where? Even that didn't bother her today.

When she was away from Salt Lake, when she had time to slow down, to think, she was sure she would remember. It was terrible, not knowing who and what she was. But somehow when she had heard the name Dale, a faint bell rang. Somewhere back in her memory was that name. Had she known someone named Dale? Had she perhaps even been in Dale itself? She had spent hours trying to remember the time before she opened her eyes in the hospital bed without identification, without memory. It had been no use.

If anyone can help me, it will be Dr. McBain. The hopeful thought left a slight smile on her lips as she entered the room. She was totally unprepared for the look in the eyes of the patient — crafty, surprised. What else did that strange gleam hold?

"April!" How had he known her name?

54

She moved to the bed, ignoring everything except the fact that he was a patient, she was a nurse.

"How can we help you?"

He stared at her disbelievingly. Had he been mistaken? And yet . . . it had to be her! She was thin beyond belief. The blue eyes held no recognition. The hair he remembered as soft brown was darker. Was it a wig? But why? Why would she be hiding behind a wig, pretending she didn't know him?

His eyes narrowed. It had to be April! He remembered the last time he had seen her and licked his lips in satisfaction. This is just what she would do. Seclude herself here, so he couldn't find her. Yet there was enough doubt for him to hold off forcing the issue.

"I'd like some dinner."

April glanced at the chart. He was scheduled for an appendectomy in the morning. She shook her head. "Sorry. We can't let you have anything now."

It seemed to enrage him. He propped himself up on one elbow. "You get me something to eat, and fast, or you'll find out I can make things plenty hot for you!"

She didn't even bother to answer, but stepped quietly from the room and reported to the floor supervisor.

The supervisor noticed the strange look

in the girl's eyes. "Is he trying to give you a bad time?"

April brushed one hand over her eyes. Before she thought she blurted out, "He's so — so odd. I feel like he is evil. I'm afraid of him."

"Do you think you might have known him before?" The floor supervisor was all attention. Let the man in 402 wait. This could be more important by far. Everyone had learned to love the girl they had named April. If she could be helped, it was priority number one.

But April was shaking her head. "I — I don't know." She shivered. "I just know I'm afraid of him."

The floor supervisor set her lips in a line that foretold trouble. "I'll take care of him." She evidently did, and in no uncertain terms. There were no further call bells from 402 that night.

April went on with her work, but part of the earlier joy had fled. If only she could remember! Alone that night in her bare room she pounded her pillow. Should she know that man? If he had known her before, how? Again the questions beat in her brain. Who am I? More importantly, what am I? Are there people somewhere looking for me, and if so, what kind of people are they?

It was a long, miserable night. But when April got back on duty the next afternoon, the patient was gone. He had gone into surgery, then been transferred to another ward.

"Good riddance!" The supervisor's tones were crisp. "I didn't like him any better than you did."

"What was his name?" April hadn't thought to check the night before. She had been too upset.

Now the supervisor looked through her charts. "Reed. Quint Reed. Does it mean anything to you?"

"No." But once more the girl shivered. "Somehow I'm glad I'll be leaving in a couple weeks. I don't feel safe here anymore."

What a strange thing to say! She didn't notice her supervisor's keen glance, or guess the woman's determination to watch April closely. If that man thought he was going to harass April in the hospital, he'd better think again!

There was no more trouble on the ward. In a few days the floor supervisor reported Quint Reed had been dismissed. For a moment the fear April had felt returned. It was heightened the next morning when she got off duty. There was a man lounging in the shadows outside the hospital. She hadn't noticed him, but as she started the short walk to her room, she could hear footsteps matched to her own, but heavier. With all her courage she refrained from looking back, but instead of going straight home, detoured down another street, a street with shops that wouldn't open for another hour, but with glass windows that would reflect. She slowed down, so did the steps. When she managed to idle by the windows she saw him . . . the stranger in the dark coat.

Was his name Quint Reed? She couldn't tell. She loitered by the windows until he must have known she had seen him, and then he quickly disappeared into an alley. Immediately April turned toward home, running. Never had she been so afraid. Gaining the safety of her own room she peered from the window.

The street was bare. He had not been able to follow her. Not that time.

But a few days later it happened again and this time from the vantage point of her window she saw him on the street in front of the hotel — a man in a dark coat, menacing because of his very stillness, looking up, up, memorizing the position of her window.

Too late April realized that although she hadn't turned on a light, he was bound to have seen light from the hall when she opened her door. The shade had not been drawn.

Waves of fear such as she had never known before poured through her. What should she do? There wasn't enough evidence to call the police. She couldn't even prove who the man was, although she strongly suspected it was their recent appendectomy patient. The fear took its toll. April began to get paler and paler.

Finally her supervisor asked, "April, you were so eager to get to Dale. Now you're upset all the time. What's happened?"

"I've been followed," she explained, her eyes wide.

"Well! Why haven't you called the police?"

But April shook her head. "And tell them what? That I'm being followed by a patient? That I'm afraid? That with everything in me I wish I could remember? I might even be married to that man, Mrs. Duffy!"

"Never!" The finality of her supervisor's voice did more toward calming April than anything else could have done. "Never in this world or any other would you be married to such as him. It's more likely he is curious, knows you've disappeared, or something."

But when April went to answer a bell,

Mrs. Duffy looked after her with a frown.

I'm glad she's leaving in just a few days. I don't like this at all.

Finally it came, the last day. There were tears in April's eyes as she told her patients good-bye, but more when she told Mrs. Duffy good-bye. She had been excused from duty that night. She needed the rest.

"Remember, if you don't like it, working with Dr. McBain, you come back here. We'll always find something for you to do."

April hugged her supervisor. "It's almost like leaving home for the first time. You know this hospital has been my home for over six months." Her laugh was shaky. "I'll hold your offer over the doctor's head so he'll have to be nice to me."

"That shouldn't be hard, looking as you do." Mrs. Duffy looked at her in approval. The new blue suit fitted beautifully. She had discarded the wig and her own hair, soft and brown, was a mass of short, fluffy curls. "You're right in style with that short hairdo."

April laughed. "It's good to have my own hair. That wig got scratchy." A shadow filled her eyes. "The blonde rinse is gone, too. I wonder why I had my hair blonde. It's always been light brown."

Mrs. Duffy was wise enough not to push

the fact April had remembered something. Let her find it on her own. But after she was gone, the busy nurse took time to watch the hospital steps. No one followed her. Perhaps it was over, the surveillance April had mentioned. Anyway, it was unlikely the man could trace her from here. Dale, Utah, was far away. With a sigh, Mrs. Duffy went back to her floor. Now if only she could find someone else as capable as her temporary helper, she would be happy.

If Mrs. Duffy could have seen April a little later that day she wouldn't have been so content. When she had finished packing, April walked to the bus station. It really wasn't that far away and she needed to get out after all the nights on duty. She would get her ticket ahead of time and not have to go down so early the next morning. It was quite a ride from Salt Lake City to Kanab.

For the last few days she had heard no footsteps, seen no dark-coated stranger outside her building. So it was with a sense of freedom, of anticipation, she walked the street. Far behind her a man followed. This time he had no dark coat but a light suit. Even if she had noticed, it wouldn't have registered with April. There was nothing about him to remind her of the furtive figure that had been haunting her.

But the man oozed satisfaction. He had seen the light brown curly hairdo with auburn lights in it. He had been right. She was the girl he thought. Taking care to keep a little distance behind her, he trailed her to the depot. Behind the shelter of a newspaper, he edged close enough to hear her crisp voice,

"One-way ticket to Kanab, please."

It was all he needed. A wicked smile crossed his face as he slipped away, but not before hearing her check the exact departure times. So she was going to Kanab. Good! The smile changed to a leer. He knew full well where she would go from there, and why. Pretty cagey, pretending she didn't know him. He'd see she would remember, and how! Maybe he could even get revenge on someone else who had wrecked his plans once upon a time. He knew that country down there well, canyons where you could be lost forever to the outside world. A daring plan crossed his mind. Why not? But in the meantime, he would try one thing more first . . .

April had been in and out all evening, getting packed, slipping down for last-minute things for her travel case. She had been careful to lock her door each time until the last trip in. She still had to go next door and tell the little old lady there good-bye. She'd only be a minute in her room. She'd just brush her hair. But as she turned to the mirror, without warning fear struck her. Why? She hadn't seen the stranger for days. Yet it was there, etching her face against the glass.

It was then the floorboard creaked and she rushed to the door. It was then the knob turned, then went into place. It was then she heard the departing footsteps, rushed to the window, and peered down. The man in the dark coat, waiting, just waiting . . . for what?

She sank to the bed, but she couldn't stand it. That stranger out there. She had to get away. With fumbling fingers she slipped out of her skirt and sweater, the only link she had with her old life, and into the blue suit, not even taking time to again admire its crisp newness.

As she dressed she planned, her mind sharpened to the keenest perception by the threat of danger in the street below. She had to get away — tonight. She couldn't stay in this room alone, frightened, watching the door for hours. Her voice cracked as she picked up the phone.

"Will you call a taxi for me please? This is room 300. I was checking out in the morning and have paid my bill. It is necessary for me to go tonight."

Then, almost as a careless afterthought, she said, "Oh, could you ask the taxi to come to the back entrance? My room's closer . . . No, I won't need any help with the bags. Will you ring when the taxi arrives? Thank you . . . What's that? A forwarding address?" She thought frantically. "Send anything in care of Mrs. Thomas Duffy."

She gave the address. Mrs. Duffy wouldn't mind and as soon as April reached Dale, she would write and explain.

It couldn't have worked out better. By the time the taxi came, April had her large case downstairs and was back up and down again with her dressing case.

It wasn't until the driver asked, "Where to, miss?" that she gasped. She hadn't even thought that far ahead in her planning. Her mind whirled. She had to give him some kind of answer. When it came it was from her subconscious.

"The hospital, please. Take me to the hospital."

He stared at her, wondering if she were sick, but something about her kept him from asking questions.

April was relieved she had evidently created no suspicion. The man had been on the street in front of her hotel when she went down the back way for the final trip. He

64

could have no way of knowing she had gone.

But when she was safely inside the hospital that had been the scene of her "second birth" to reality, her knees trembled, and as Mrs. Duffy's eyes opened wide to see April there at that time of night, it was too much. The distraught girl dropped her luggage and flew straight to her floor supervisor. Fortunately no one else was in sight.

"Mrs. Duffy, hide me somewhere until tomorrow morning and I can get away!" In whispers she told what had happened. "If only I knew what he wanted! I almost felt like rushing down and demanding he tell me. But I'm afraid, so afraid."

Mrs. Duffy was filled with pity. How terrible it must be not to know who you were, or why a strange man was following you!

"Don't you worry, April. There's an empty room at the end of the hall. You can slip in there. I'll get you up on time to get your bus."

She got April to the room and finished off by hanging a *Do Not Disturb* sign on the door.

"There. That will keep our nurses from coming in. I'll tell them we've got a new patient while they were on break. Thank heavens it's quiet tonight!"

Her matter-of-fact manner quieted April,

65

along with the security of the hospital itself. But her parting words steadied the girl more than anything else.

"As soon as you get to Dale, you'll be safe, April. Dr. McBain will see to that." With a rustle of starched skirts, Mrs. Duffy was gone, leaving comfort in the room.

Dr. McBain. Of course. April visualized his red hair, his massive build, his aggressive approach to life. No one could harm her with Dr. McBain around. Suddenly the worry, the tension, the fear, drained from her, leaving her tireder than she had ever been before. Dr. McBain would take care of her. Tomorrow she would be there. Safe, secure, unthreatened.

April, the girl who could not remember, slept.

Chapter 5

The low sobbing went on and on, muffled by Autumn's pillow. Not for anything must April, asleep in her own room next door, hear Autumn's heartbreak. The miserable girl reviewed the day in her mind, the day starting so gloriously happy.

"She's coming, Letty. She's coming today!"

Never had Letty seen Autumn's face so radiant in all the years she had known her. For a moment she was tempted to warn her, to caution Autumn not to expect too much. But she didn't have the heart to do it, to dim the brightness of the expectant girl.

Autumn didn't notice the older woman's silence as she chattered on. "Her room's all ready. Just the way she left it. I know when she sees it she's bound to remember."

Letty made a choked sound but said nothing. Autumn didn't even catch it. She was too lost in her own world, the world of a returning twin sister.

"Even if she doesn't recognize the room, she'll know me." How confident she had been!

Finally Letty knew she had to say, "Remember, Autumn, it may not be our April." The words had hung in the air, but Autumn refused to recognize them.

"She is, Letty. I know she is." She whirled around the kitchen, then dashed for the door. "I'm too excited to eat." She paused, her face darkening. "I can't see why I couldn't go to Kanab with Dr. McBain to get April."

Letty had overheard the argument the day before. Wisely she didn't comment but remembered it well.

"It's my right. She's my sister!" Autumn's temper could match her reddish hair, although she usually controlled it.

Dr. McBain's temper had been even hotter, triggered by uncertainty. Maybe he wasn't doing right, bringing April here. What if she was a stranger? In spite of Autumn's assurance of welcome, he knew how disappointed she would be. Now his answer was short.

"Is she? We don't know that. It isn't your right, anyway. To her you're a stranger."

"But she'll know me — I know she will!"

Dr. McBain carefully counted ten, then exploded anyway. "That's exactly what we don't know! She may not know you from Adam. She's got to find her way back without your interference, do you hear me?" He was roaring.

Autumn's reply was icy. "I could hardly fail to hear you, the way you're shouting."

"I mean what I say, Nurse Dale."

Part of the girl's mind registered, *So we're back to Nurse Dale. I wonder if it's because she is coming.* But her chin only tilted higher.

"I have no intention of forcing her into any kind of recognition. But I still know she will recognize me."

Dr. McBain threw up his hands and strode out of the office, leaving an angry, red-faced nurse behind. There had been a coolness between them for the rest of the day.

Now Autumn's lips turned up in a smile. *Dr. McBain will see. April's going to know me.*

Endless hours followed one another that day for both Autumn and Letty. Dr. McBain left in the afternoon to get April. The patients had all been dismissed to their own homes, and after doing a few rounds for injections and the like Autumn was free.

It was the last thing she needed, freedom

and time to think. She and Letty, with Maxine's help, had been so busy since they knew April was coming, there had been little time to worry. Now she had to face it. What if it really wasn't April? Autumn licked her lips nervously. She had meant what she said about taking the girl in and helping her. But what a terrible shock it would be!

I shouldn't have let myself count so much on it. But it was too late. She could see Dr. McBain's car driving into the curving driveway in front of the house. For a moment Autumn closed her eyes, steeling herself against disappointment. Then she opened them and looked from the window before running to the door.

Dr. McBain was helping a girl in a blue suit get out of the car. A girl with light brown fluffy curls. A girl with blue eyes, and a thin face. A girl who looked up at her own home without recognition. A girl named April — Autumn's twin. But the blank stare at the house had warned Autumn. She summoned every bit of courage and calmness gained from her nurses' training and went to the door.

April saw the door open and a beautiful girl step through, a girl with a welcoming smile. Her heart lifted. How nice! She knew

70

automatically she would enjoy sharing quarters with her.

April didn't notice the quiver in Dr. McBain's voice as he said, "This is Autumn Dale."

Autumn held out her hand and April took it, noticing its coldness. Why, the other girl was shivering! Was she ill?

Trying to ease over the moment April said, "Autumn Dale. What a pretty name! We ought to get along well, April and Autumn."

It was almost too much. Autumn bit her lip to hold back tears, tears of terrible disappointment. *Grown women, especially nurses, don't cry, and in front of their patients.* The thought had come unbidden, yet Autumn recognized her flash of insight. April would be a patient until the cloud covering her mind was lifted. It was her duty and responsibility to provide the love and warmth to see that cloud did lift. Suddenly Autumn realized she had been silent far too long. There was a question in April's eyes. Did she feel unwelcome? The thought loosened Autumn's frozen tongue.

"Come in, April, Dr. McBain. April, we're so glad to have you here." She led the way through the living room into the kitchen. Letty, bless her heart, was busy with dinner pots and pans. "Dinner will be ready. Would you like to wash up?"

Before April could answer, Autumn turned back to Dr. McBain. "Would you like to stay? It's pot roast."

His forced heartiness dispelled the last doubt. His laugh boomed. "For Letty's pot roast I'd not only stay but eat seconds!"

In a wave of laughter Autumn took her sister upstairs. Upstairs to April's own suite of bedroom and small bath. She held her breath, noticing how April looked around, as if puzzled, before her face lighted.

"Oh, it's yellow! I always loved yellow."

Well, at least it was something, if not the recognition Autumn had hoped for. On impulse she put her arm around the thin shoulders. "We're glad you're here, April. Letty and I would just rattle around in this big house."

There was a suspicious moisture in April's eyes. "I'm glad you want me." She swallowed. "I suppose you know I don't know who I am or —"

Autumn couldn't stand the forlorn note in April's voice. She deliberately interrupted. "So what? There are days I'm sure we get so busy none of us know exactly who we are around here. Besides" — she gestured toward the window, framing a gorgeous sunset and a lone cottonwood swaying in the light breeze — "a few months of this and you'll be ready to remember everything." She was unprepared for the swiftness of April's reply.

"Thank you, Autumn Dale."

Quickly Autumn turned away to hide the quick rush of feeling. She remembered Dr. McBain's words:

". . . without your interference, you hear me?" He was right.

"Supper will be getting cold." Autumn laughed. "You know, I usually call it dinner, Letty calls it supper, so you'll have to answer to both."

"Gladly!" April had run a comb through her curls and was ready to follow Autumn downstairs.

Their meal bordered on the hilarious, with each trying to make the others feel at ease. Dr. McBain regaled April with an account of his first ride-out call and the resulting poison oak. Letty and Autumn assured her the doctor was a better doctor than he was a patient, and all three did everything they could to make the poor, lost lamb feel at home. They succeeded above and beyond their wildest expectations.

When Dr. McBain rose to go, April startled them all, saying, "If ever I find out who

I am it will be here." She looked directly into Dr. McBain's eyes, then at Letty, last of all at Autumn. "And if I don't, well, I'll just stay here with all of you!"

It was Letty who first found her voice. "That would suit us just fine, April. Now in the meantime, why don't you walk over to the hospital with the doctor? It's still early. Autumn and I will do the dishes."

"But I want to help. If I'm going to live with you, I want to do my full share."

"Oh, you will, don't worry about that! But for the first few days, until you become familiar with the routine, don't worry about it."

Only half-convinced, April followed the doctor out the door. Vowing never to be a nuisance in her new home, she looked back with a smile and a wave for the two who loved her so much. If she had known how very welcome she was, how much they longed for her to remember, it might have unsettled her. But she happily trotted along beside the tall doctor, asking questions.

From the doorway Autumn watched them go. She didn't realize Letty had not gone into the kitchen. If she had, Autumn would never have let her expression slip as it did. It hurt to watch Dr. McBain and her unsuspecting twin laughing together.

Why didn't he laugh like that with her, Autumn? *I'm glad,* she thought fiercely, *I'm glad he likes her a lot. She needs him more than I do.* It was the first time Autumn admitted even to herself that her interest in the doctor went beyond her admiration for his medical skills. She refused to think about it.

But Letty had seen the look in her eyes, changing from wistfulness to determination. Quietly she slipped away before Autumn would discover her there. She knew Autumn had begun to care for Dr. McBain, perhaps even more than the girl herself knew. It was with a sigh she began the dishes, hiding her feelings when Autumn came out to help.

"It isn't going to be easy," the older woman said.

Autumn dropped her dishtowel, a wave of color flushing her face. Had Letty guessed her thoughts? "Wha . . . what do you mean?"

"It isn't going to be easy pretending she's just someone who's come to live with us. We're going to have to watch every word, every chance move that might give it all away."

Autumn's heart was filled with relief. She didn't even want Letty to think that she . . . that . . . "We have to do it!" Her voice was determined. "She has to come back on her own. We can't push her into false remembering, just because we want it that way."

Letty nodded. "That's exactly what I mean. It would be simple to mention something to hurry her along." Her face was serious. "We'll just have to love her and give her a home." There were sudden tears in her eyes.

"Thank you, Letty." Autumn's words said so much more. The appreciation for Letty leaving her own little home, for living with them to help April, for all the things she was. It was only the knowledge of Letty's strength to fall back on that kept Autumn going brightly until bedtime. She kept it up until she was alone in her room, door closed. Then the sobbing had begun. She knew it was nervous reaction. She also knew it was better to get it out of her system so she could face the next day, and the next, and the next. But she wasn't prepared for the sudden opening of the door, or the soft, thin hand that touched her tear-wet cheek.

"Autumn." The voice was hesitant, unwilling to intrude. "Are you sick? Can I help?"

It was almost too much. For one wild moment Autumn felt like flinging herself into April's arms and telling her the whole story. But she couldn't. It was the worst thing she could do.

"No," she choked. "I'm all right." She frantically cast around in her mind for a logical explanation. A thought came. Did she dare? Did she dare go so far and no further? Grim determination swept through her.

"You see, I had a sister once, a twin — and I lost her. Sometimes I miss her terribly. We used to share everything. She looked a little as you look." Autumn held her breath.

The little hand had stilled. But April's voice was natural. "I had a sister, too, once . . ." Her voice trailed off uncertainly. "Could I . . . do you suppose we could be sisters? I know it's kind of childlike, but I need to belong, Autumn. Since I've come here I've had the strangest feeling of belonging. I've even remembered a few things. That I like the color yellow. That I had a sister." She paused. "If only I could remember more!"

In an instant Autumn was all nurse. She shoved back her own leap of excitement in her concern for April, still a patient.

"Don't try to push it, April. You will remember. Probably a little bit at a time. Just don't try to hurry it. Dr. McBain says it's best not to force yourself." She could feel the relaxation go through her twin.

"Dr. McBain. Autumn, you'll never know what he's done for me." The gratitude in her voice colored it highly. All Autumn heard was the praise. "I really didn't even care when I first woke up in that strange hospital. Strange faces, noises. Where was I? Who was I? I was terrified."

Autumn felt as if she were going through the experience.

"No one could tell me anything. I was desperate. Then Dr. McBain came. He encouraged me, as soon as I was able, to help in the hospital in small ways. He looked after me and made me learn to laugh again. If I lived to be a thousand, I could never repay Dr. McBain for what he did. He literally saved my life. I had come to the point where it seemed useless to live in an unknown world."

Her voice dropped a little lower yet was still clear. "The best thing he did was bring me here. I have a feeling you are right. Now I guess all I need is patience."

It was an opening. Autumn remembered something April used to say and she quoted it. "There was a man who needed patience so he prayed for it. 'Lord, give me patience — and give it to me right now!'"

April giggled. "That sounds like me!" She stepped away, then turned back. The light from the hall streamed through the door.

"Good night, Autumn."

"Good night, April — sister."

Another moment and she was gone, leaving a shaken Autumn more unable to sleep than she had been before. When she was sure April was in her own room, Autumn turned on her bedside light. Dr. McBain would want to know what had been said tonight, every word of it. If she waited until morning she might not remember.

Carefully she wrote down the conversation, not omitting even one word. But when she was finished, she was still restless. Slipping into a robe, she felt her way to the chair by her window, the window looking out under the crisp moonlit night to the big red-rock mountain at the edge of town. The breeze coming in the open window was cool, and she wrapped her robe closer, trying to sort out all her feelings of the day. It wasn't easy. As Letty had said, they would have to watch themselves. Tonight she had gone further than she had thought possible. Dr. McBain probably wouldn't approve.

Dr. McBain. Autumn thought of his tender look of compassion for April at dinner, reading into it more than was actually there. She remembered April's impassioned words. "If I lived to be a thousand I could never repay Dr. McBain for what he did. He literally saved my life."

Tension filled Autumn. Nothing must stand in the way of April's recovery, nothing. If Dr. McBain was the one to help her make that recovery, that's the way it would have to be. Autumn's slim shoulders felt bent beneath the double strain, the strain of having her beloved twin sister asleep in the next room and knowing that same twin cared a great deal for Dr. Matthew McBain.

For an instant Autumn relived that day when she had cried her heart out against his broad chest, taking comfort in the remembrance of the strong arms that had held her safe. And yet those same strong arms could protect April. April, who needed shelter much more than she herself needed it. April, the frail one. April, adrift on an ocean of forgetfulness. April, whose very face lit up at the thought of Matthew McBain.

It was a long, hard fight for the exhausted girl. For hours Autumn sat by the window, watching the night, reveling in its beauty while rejecting its comfort. She hadn't realized how deep her feelings had grown even in the short time since he had come.

At one point she lifted her face to the cold, uncaring moon, silently asking, "Why? Why did I have to meet him and learn to care, only to lose him — before he ever knew how I felt?"

And yet a few moments later she knew she was glad. Never must he suspect that for those last days her attachment had become so personal, so all-encompassing. She hadn't even known it herself; she had been too worried about April's arrival. He must never know. The shapely head covered with red-gold hair lifted proudly.

When he had laughingly asked her, "And how about Nurse Autumn Dale? Does she have any immediate matrimonial plans?" she had replied she didn't have any. It had been because she meant it. The loss of her parents, the disappearance of April after April's fiance's treachery — all had combined to convince her she would be happier going through life alone. It hurt too much to care.

Now the girl at the window knew something else. It was worth it. Caring, loving, pain. Intermingled. Tomorrow she would tear it out of her heart and life forever, step aside spiritually as well as physically, so April and Dr. McBain could discover each other. But for this one night she knew all the wonder of recalling a tall, craggy doctor with green eyes, red hair, and a temper to match.

Autumn knew something else. She had gone to the window a girl, carrying with her all her dreams of Sir Galahad, Lancelot, every storybook character, every knight in shining armor. During the long night hours she had put aside those dreams, carefully burying them in her love for someone else, and that someone else's need. Only she would ever know what it cost her to unselfishly, even gladly, step out of the picture in favor of April. She didn't think of it as an atonement, a making up to April for a time when an unfaithful fiance had attempted to use her own sister as the object of his careless attentions. Yet perhaps it was. April had been shattered once, but never again. And especially not on Autumn's account.

Early dawn fingers were stretching, reaching into the sky before Autumn crawled back in bed, shivering from the night air. But she was no huddled, miserable figure. She had fought her fight and come out triumphant. She could face whatever she had to face. For in the time of decision she had not only put aside girlhood dreams, she had also put aside girlhood. The Autumn Dale who would take up her nursing duties the following morning had become a woman.

Chapter 6

Autumn stopped in her rush down the hall for a brief word with April.

"Boy, is this ever the baby season!" Autumn said.

"I know what you mean. One yesterday, one today, and another expected in tomorrow. Are they synchronized, or something?"

Autumn's hands were already reaching in the supply closet for more packages of sterile cloth. "They must be. But it's fun, isn't it?"

April's eyes glowed. Even in the few days she had been in Dale, her thin cheeks had begun to fill out. Letty made sure there was plenty of good food and that the cookie jar was full. April was surprised at her own appetite, but the others only laughed at her.

"It will do you good. Get some meat on your bones," Letty said. April had taken to the hospital work immediately. But then, why shouldn't she? In the days before her accident, she had been a crackerjack nurse.

Now as they showed her various procedures she would get partway through and tell them, "I know how from here." And she'd go on to do an expert butterfly bandage, or limb strapping, or whatever it was she was learning. Finally one day she commented, "I must have been a nurse or at least have had some training. First aid or something."

Dr. McBain glanced at her across the table. "Yes, you must have been."

He could see improvement in April since she came. He also noticed something else. While Autumn was thrilled to have her sister there in Dale, working alongside her on routine duties, something was bothering her. She was just as efficient, maybe even more so. She was just as tender toward her patients. But she was different toward him. Perversely he missed the spunky girl who had stood up for her rights, when he used to give her a bad time.

A few times he even approached her. "Is something wrong, Nurse Dale . . . Autumn?"

Her answer was cool. "Nothing whatsoever, Dr. McBain."

It left him baffled. He traced it back to the

arrival of April but couldn't figure out why. Sure, Autumn was disappointed that April's memory hadn't returned faster, but why should it change her attitude toward him? Yet there wasn't much time for reflection. April's arrival had seemed to be the signal. One thing after another happened and the little hospital was bursting to overflowing. Now, as Autumn had said, it was baby season. The first had been yesterday, a relatively easy birth.

"It ought to be," the big farm woman told them, chuckling. "It will be my seventh!" Her prediction had been right. She hadn't been in the hospital an hour before her daughter was born, a welcome addition to the six strapping sons they already had in their family.

"She'll be spoiled rotten." Autumn smiled, holding up the baby for the mother to see. She carefully instructed and watched April clean up the tiny mite, then gently lay it in the mother's waiting arms. "What are you going to name her?"

The woman looked shamefaced, then pulled Autumn closer and beckoned April near the bed. "I'm going to name her Faith."

"Why, that's a beautiful name!"

But the new mother laughed. "Don't ever tell anyone why. But you'll get a kick out of it. I wanted a daughter so badly." She grinned and added quickly, "Not that I don't love my six boys. But it would be nice to have a little girl. So I just made up my mind it was going to be a girl, and every time I thought about it I decided to have faith. Her name is Faith."

Autumn and April exchanged glances. Amusement mingled with feeling for this woman who had wanted a baby daughter.

"We won't tell, and she's lovely." She was. Rosy, round, beautiful, with a mop of dark hair inclined to curl.

Now little Faith nestled in her mother's arms, content with the strange new world she had recently entered.

Suddenly Autumn's face was serious. "April, I'm worried about today's baby. Mrs. Jimson is so tired and rundown. Dr. McBain is afraid of toxemia poisoning in the bloodstream. Besides, he's going to have to do a Caesarean section. The baby's in such a poor position it couldn't be born naturally. He wanted Mrs. Jimson to go to Kanab where they have better facilities, but she wouldn't. She almost didn't consent to coming in here. She said her other baby was born at home. Why couldn't this one be? It wasn't until Dr. McBain reminded her the other one didn't live that she finally agreed to come. I'm afraid we're in for some pretty rough going."

Autumn's prediction was true. Mrs. Jimson *was* rundown. She had no idea where Mr. Jimson was. He was fond of taking off every so often and returning when he got ready. But this time she needed him. She needed to know someone really cared about her. Being denied that security she hadn't taken the trouble to eat properly. Now her baby would suffer from it.

Dr. McBain shook his head as he met Autumn's eyes. They were all set up, ready to go. Maxine Phillips had been called in to assist. Autumn was serving as anesthetist. And April would stand back ready to get anything else they might need. It was April's first time in surgery. If everyone hadn't been so worried about the patient, they might have noticed the competent way she moved, careful to stay out of the way, yet alert to any commands. Once she had tied the surgical gowns for the others and fastened their masks, she stepped back.

It was also the first time Autumn had watched Dr. McBain operate. He was not only fast, he was decisive. From the first incision, to the removal of the baby, through the final careful finish, his actions were smooth. There wasn't one wasted motion.

April had been handed the baby, but as soon as Autumn saw Mrs. Jimson was starting to come out of the anesthetic, she slipped to April's side.

"Poor little mite!" Autumn said. It was true. Mrs. Jimson had also delivered a girl, but what a difference. This one was scrawny, a little chicken, with blue-tinged eyelids. She breathed, but just once. Life for her was not a happy thing. It was easier to give up before she ever really lived. There were tears in the twins' eyes as they silently cared for the tiny body. Dr. McBain had taken in at a glance what had happened. It was he who was right there by Mrs. Jimson's side when she regained consciousness. In a low voice he told her about the baby. He might as well have saved his breath.

Her voice was flat as she said, "I don't believe it."

Dr. McBain almost dropped the syringe he had prepared. But in another moment he plunged it into her arm. Better for her to sleep until some of the pain was over. He didn't want her threshing around, not with the incision needing to heal. When she was fully aware, he would talk with her again, make her understand.

Seldom in his career had Dr. McBain come across a woman like Mrs. Jimson. For one thing, he couldn't know that in spite of her lack of care for herself, she had looked forward to this baby more than anything else in the world. She had lost her first one. That he knew. But he could not know that all the love she had once given her husband had been channeled into the prospect of being a mother, with a baby who couldn't go away and leave her.

Now her baby had done just that. It was enough to bring her to the edge of sanity, teetering on the brink. The fact that she saw another mother in the second bed in maternity, a mother nursing a healthy, rosy little girl-baby, proved to be her undoing.

Mrs. Jimson didn't say anything, didn't speak one word beyond that initial, "I don't believe it." But in the next few days she watched. She listened. She found out the farm woman's name was Annie Wells. She watched little Faith, and in her twisted mind a plan began to grow.

Autumn's heart ached for the poor woman even though she had no way of knowing to what desperate lengths the twisted mind would go. It was Autumn who told Annie Wells about Mrs. Jimson and her loss. She had counted on the warmhearted generosity of Mrs. Wells.

"Would you like to hold Faith?"

Mrs. Jimson couldn't speak, but her outstretched arms were answer enough.

Carefully Autumn transferred the little girl from her mother's arms to Mrs. Jimson's. As Mrs. Jimson looked down, a great sob rose in her throat. It told the other two women more than she could have done any other way.

Every day Mrs. Jimson held Faith. But neither Autumn nor Mrs. Wells knew what she had decided.

"Going-home day for you!" Autumn smiled at Annie Wells. She was glad Dr. Archer and Dr. McBain believed in keeping mothers a bit longer in the hospital than some of the city hospitals where in a day or two they were dismissed. If she hadn't been too busy helping Annie get ready, bundling up Faith, she might have noticed Mrs. Jimson's eyes.

April noticed. She had been in the background, just watching. She never knew what caused her to suddenly shift her gaze to Mrs. Jimson, but in that quick flash she saw the pain, the hurt, almost a madness that came into the woman's face as Mrs. Wells stepped out the door with Faith, turning back to wave good-bye to them. It was enough for her to call Autumn aside.

"I think you should watch Mrs. Jimson. She looked absolutely insane when they left."

Autumn looked up, startled. "Insane?"

"Yes. You know, as if Faith were her baby."

There was silence between them. Then Autumn swung back into the room.

"Well, Mrs. Jimson. You'll be next to go home." Ignoring the woman's continued silence, she chattered away, smoothing her pillows, straightening her sheets. April had stripped the bed across the way and Autumn saw Mrs. Jimson's eyes dart there. *April had been right. This woman's mind was on the verge of madness.*

"I'm going to see Dr. McBain about the patient we were discussing," Autumn said.

April's eyes met Autumn's in understanding, but she only nodded. Autumn walked swiftly toward the office, but before she could get there, an excited man rushed in.

"Nurse, my wife. This time it's for real."

Autumn bit back a smile. His wife was the third of the baby trio they had expected. It was their first child, and the morning had come and gone without labor pains. They had been so positive of the day the baby would come! But now his face showed this was really it.

"Bring her in here." Autumn's orders were crisp.

April had finished the bed and come back for her next assignment.

"Get Dr. McBain. Number three is just about to arrive."

It was a different case than either of the others. Outside of the baby's father being so nervous, everything went off fine. The young couple had been through the prenatal training class and he stayed in the delivery room. The mother was calm, and when the first cry sounded, she smiled. But the *thud* behind Autumn caused her to whirl and stare disbelievingly at the floor. The brand-new father was slumped there. He had come through with flying colors — until it was all over!

Dr. McBain snorted, then hid it with a cough at Autumn's glare. She helped the new father to a chair, easing his embarrassment by showing off his little son. But the climax came when both father and baby had been ushered out.

The wife giggled. "Poor dear. It's been quite an ordeal for him!"

A second later all three of them were laughing in great gulps. Autumn could hardly wait to tell April the aftermath. But when she went out, there was no sign of April, just a note:

"I'M IN MRS. JIMSON'S ROOM."

There was nothing in the few words to alarm Autumn, but a tingle ran through her. She remembered how she had rushed out to tell Dr. McBain about Mrs. Jimson. Then the new maternity case had come in. Now that Maxine had taken the baby to prepare it for mama's arms, the other worry rushed back.

"Oh, dear!" Autumn reached Mrs. Jimson's room in a flash. It was too late. April was standing staring at the bed, a bed that was tossed back carelessly, sheets halfway to the floor, the pillow at the foot. An empty bed that had held a woman who lost her baby.

Autumn said, "Get Dr. McBain."

In a moment he was there, April's white face behind him.

"She's gone," Autumn said. "We also believe she may be a little mad."

In a few words they told Dr. McBain what had only been noticed that day.

At first he was inclined to think it was a passing thing. "She'll probably just go home and forget it all."

"Then why didn't she wait until she was released?" Autumn asked.

He shrugged, giving the appearance of noncommittal disinterest.

Autumn sighed thoughtfully. "Dr. McBain, that woman could be dangerous."

April nodded. "I think so, too. There was a look in her eyes as she watched Mrs. Wells leave with Faith . . ." She broke off, shuddering.

The doctor looked at them keenly. Even though he hadn't noticed anything unusual about the woman except her initial reaction, he said, "I don't believe it." He didn't like what he was hearing from the girls.

"How long has she been gone, does anyone know?" Autumn glanced at her watch. "Let's see. It was about eleven when Mrs. Wells left. It's after one now. That means if Mrs. Jimson left when we went out of the room, she has over two hours' start." Her look was direct, her voice even as she added, "Plenty of time to get to the Wells place — and away again."

"Oh, come now, Nurse Dale. You don't really mean you think Mrs. Jimson is capable of stealing another woman's child!"

"That's exactly what I think."

They stared at one another. Dr. McBain's head was whirling. He had never seen Autumn so stubborn, so almost defiant. It convinced him.

"Go call the Wellses right away."

"There's no need to call them."

All three turned to the doorway. Maxine Phillips stood there, her face white. "After I took the new baby back to his mother, the phone rang." She clutched the doorframe as if for support. "It was Mrs. Wells. Her baby has disappeared."

Maxine swallowed hard. "Mrs. Jimson came to see her this morning, just dropped in, she said. She was holding Faith when suddenly Mrs. Jimson asked if she might have a glass of water. You know how hospitable Mrs. Wells is. Instead of water, she took the time to make coffee and get out some fresh cookies. When she got back, Mrs. Jimson was gone — with Faith, evidently. Annie thought at first they might just have stepped outside. She didn't really believe the woman would just take Faith and go. But after her husband and the other men searched the whole place, she had to face it. Mrs. Jimson had stolen Faith! That's why she called us."

It was a grim-faced Matthew McBain who ordered, "Autumn, get my kit. We're going out to Jimson's now!"

In moments they were rattling over the hot, dusty road.

"What are we going to do when we get there?" Autumn asked.

"First we have to get there before Mr. Wells and his men!"

Matt McBain was right. There was no telling what a woman in Mrs. Jimson's condition might do if confronted with a band of men coming after the baby she probably thought in her contorted mind was her own.

In reality it was only a short drive to the old house where the Jimsons lived. But in the nightmare surrounding them, it seemed hours before they reached it. Not a breeze stirred. No sign of life at all. And then, from the shadowy depths beyond a dirty window, something moved.

Dr. McBain and Autumn had been careful to park their jeep around the bend where it couldn't be seen from the house. They had crept up the back way, working their way behind stunted cedars and huge rocks in fantastic red shapes. They had a clear view of the cabin as well as the road.

"I'm going back down the road to head off the search party," the doctor said.

In a moment he was gone, leaving Autumn behind the scanty shelter. She knew he would want her to stay there, and yet . . . a wild idea had crossed her mind.

Standing in plain sight, clutching the doctor's bag in front of her so it was visible, she called, "Mrs. Jimson!"

The only answer was a shatter of dirty glass. Then something long and rusty poked through the broken window. "Stay where you are!" It was a rifle. Would one that old really shoot?

It was a chance Autumn would have to take.

With every ounce of courage she could muster, she put authority in her voice. "Mrs. Jimson, open the door, please. It's about the baby."

The cackle that answered was fair warning. It was insane.

"My baby! No one's going to take my baby! They went away, him, everyone. But my baby isn't going to go away and leave me!"

Cold chills went down Autumn's spine, but no colder than those going through Dr. McBain's system as he stepped to the top of the rise and saw Autumn calmly walking toward that window — and the rifle. Fear clutched his throat, fear for the girl whose hair shone in the sunlight. He couldn't speak, call out. It was just as well. Motioning back the others, whom he had intercepted on their way up the old road, he stood still, watching.

"Mrs. Jimson, please open the door. I've brought the baby's formula." Would her ruse work? For a long moment Autumn thought not. She added persuasively, "Little

Faith is bound to be hungry. It's long past her usual feeding time."

As if to reiterate Autumn's words the baby let out a long wail. It turned the trick.

The rifle barrel wavered, then disappeared. Another long moment of waiting. Another wail from the baby. Then a slow, creaking of a key in a rusty lock, and an opening door.

Autumn stepped into the dark, littered cabin. The musty smell hit her in the face. It had been closed while Mrs. Jimson was in the hospital. She could see the beady eyes of the maddened woman staring at her.

"Thank you, Mrs. Jimson." She glanced around. "My, it's dark in here, isn't it?" She deliberately pushed the door wide open, hoping Dr. McBain would understand her signal. She raised her voice. "We'll just shove this old gun over in the corner. We don't need it, do we?" *Force yourself to smile. Act naturally.* It was the hardest advice she'd ever given herself.

"Now, let's feed Faith, Mrs. Jimson." She reached in the doctor's bag, carefully withdrawing the hastily filled bottle, hoping she wouldn't have to feed Faith. Faith was a breast-fed baby. She might not even take the bottle.

Autumn never knew. In the moments she

took Faith from the reluctant arms and fussed with the bottle, Mrs. Jimson's entire attention was on her. The distracted woman never knew when foreign eyes peered through the window, or when men on silent feet slipped to the porch. She was so busy watching Autumn with "her" baby, for a moment the insane woman had forgotten everything else.

Then it was over. The swift rush of many feet into the darkened cabin. The firm but gentle seizing of the creature whose only crime had been prompted by mother love. The sudden collapse of the tired woman, both physically and mentally, and it was over. She would be taken where she could be helped. In the meantime Annie Wells waited just down the road around the corner for her baby girl.

That evening April and Autumn sat alone on the front porch. Letty was on duty with the new little mother, and the other patients in Big Rock Hospital. The twins were silent, enjoying one of the last evenings that would be warm enough to sit outside.

"If you hadn't noticed the look in her eyes . . ." Autumn's voice was solemn.

"But if you hadn't known what to do. Oh, Autumn, what if she'd shot you?"

Autumn shook her head. "I don't think

she could have, April. Mrs. Jimson was over the brink thinking about a baby girl. But she didn't have it in her to murder anyone. She just wanted someone to love."

"Don't we all?" April's voice was quiet, and she stood to go inside.

Long after things were quiet for the night, Autumn thought of her twin's words. Was April longing for love, for Dr. McBain's love, perhaps? It didn't hurt so much as it had before. Autumn had forced her own feelings back until she felt she was in control.

Yet the very next morning she had the battle to fight all over again.

Chapter 7

Autumn should have been warned by the storm signals in Dr. McBain's green eyes.

He snapped, "Nurse Dale, I want to see you in my office."

She looked up in surprise and followed him, leaving a staring April behind. Silently she took the chair he indicated, then just waited.

The storm broke immediately. "Of all the fool performances I ever saw, yours yesterday takes top prize!"

It was the last thing she had expected from him. Yesterday? Oh, yes. The kidnapping. Somehow it seemed days ago, instead of hours.

"There didn't seem to be anything else to do."

Her very quietness enraged him more. "There had to be another way. You could have been killed! Didn't you think of that?"

For a moment Autumn closed her eyes, feeling the pang of fear she had felt when that long rifle barrel came through the window, pointing at her.

"I thought of it."

Matt McBain's big fist crashed on the desk. "Then why, in the name of heaven, did you rush in there like a heroine in a dime novel?"

Autumn almost told him, *There are no dime novels anymore — they're more like two dollars.* Just in time she bit her lip. How could she think of such a thing when he was so serious? Instead she leaned forward, her own eyes sea-green and cool.

"There was the life of a baby involved, a baby named Faith. What do you think would have happened if you and your crew had rushed in that cabin? How would she have reacted, the woman who had gone mad from the loss of her own child? I couldn't take the chance on her, not knowing what she would do. Do you think I *wanted* to go in there? You must be out of your mind! I was scared, more scared than I've ever been before in my whole life.

"But I had to go. I'm a nurse, Dr. McBain, dedicated to the saving of life. It was my duty. All the fear in the world couldn't have kept me from doing what I felt I had to do.

Call it stupidity, or call it faith that I would be protected — your choice. Whatever you call it, there was nothing else I could do except exactly what I did."

She paused for a great gulp of air. "And furthermore, Dr. McBain, while we're on the subject, if I were in the same circumstances tomorrow, or the day after that, or next week or next month or next year, *I would do the very same thing again if I had to!*" Her beautiful hair swung around her flushed face. She hadn't been so lovely since he came. Suddenly all the good doctor's anger was gone.

Before Autumn knew what was happening, he was out from behind the desk and had her in his arms. The iron bands of control he had set on himself, the determination not to tell her how he had fallen in love with her when he first came — all were lost.

He had spent a sleepless night, thinking over and over again of that terrible moment when he had seen the rifle in the hands of a madwoman pointed at Autumn. Cold sweat had run down his face. He knew if anything had happened to her, life for him would be worthless, without meaning.

"If you had died, Autumn . . ." His voice choked off. Then his mouth was coming down on her own, and she responded. For long moments they stood there. Her two hands crept back of his neck, clinging to him, to his strength, his concern. Then she remembered April.

It took Matt McBain time to realize his kisses were no longer being returned, that she was struggling for freedom, hair disheveled, eyes bright. He looked at her blankly. What had brought on the change?

"You mustn't, you mustn't!" She was straining away from him.

But he brought her back. "Why not, Autumn? I love you. You must know that. When I saw that woman pointing her rifle at you, I wanted to leap in front of it, strike her to the ground. I'll take care of you, Autumn. I love you."

But she jerked away and put her hands over her ears. "I won't listen!"

He stared disbelievingly. Surely he hadn't imagined the warm response of just moments ago. It had been heaven. His eyes narrowed. With one stride he had her hands in his, away from her ears.

"You will listen, Autumn Dale! I'm not a teenage kid, spouting love and devotion. I'm a grown man. Whether you like it or not, I'm in love with you and it's for keeps, not some stupid game. Someday you are going to marry me. You may as well know it right now."

"I am not!"

"Oh, yes, you are. It may take a long time but someday you're going to be my wife. We're going to work together, and laugh and love and share life itself. We're going to dream dreams, and make those dreams of a better world come true, using our skills. I don't know when. I won't push you, at least not too much. But you might as well get used to the idea."

She was very still. Only her high color showed she had heard. But her ragged breathing gave her away. Dr. McBain knew in that moment she did care, a great deal. Then what was it? An idea flashed on like a brilliant light.

"Is it April?"

Autumn nodded slowly. "Yes — it's April."

There was no way of knowing their meanings were diametrically opposed. Matt McBain took Autumn's reticence for concern for her sister, worry over the future. Autumn had intended him to take it that way. His nearness had shattered all her carefully built defenses. They lay at her feet. She felt any resistance she could offer would be no more protection than a cardboard sword.

She had no intention of telling him April loved him, or that it was better that way. She couldn't. Not after this stormy session. Inside, a little voice whispered gloriously, *He loves you, he loves you!* She firmly ignored it and looked straight in his eyes.

"She needs all the help she can get."

Dr. McBain's shoulders slumped. Then with a crooked grin he retreated back to the desk. "So I told you I wasn't going to push you — at least not too much." Then, after a minute of silent watching, he said, "Of course, if you can look me in the eyes and tell me you don't care for me, or never will care for me, it could make a difference in my attitude."

She stared at him. He was offering her a way out. They both knew she couldn't take it. There was no way in the world she could lie to those bright green eyes that saw through a reluctant sweetheart with all the keen perception gained from seeing through malingering patients. But maybe, just maybe, there was another way. Autumn stood and smoothed her uniform and hair, desperately playing against time to compose herself. When she spoke, it was with her usual cool tones.

"I wouldn't so lower myself as to do such a childish thing."

Before he could recover from his surprise, she had gone, leaving Matthew McBain shaken. He hadn't expected such poise from her, especially in the face of his impossible test. What an opponent, a worthy opponent! When swords clashed, hers was strong and true. He tilted the chair back until it squeaked in protest, a little smile coming across his face.

Let her play her little game. After all, she was only twenty-one. Let her take her time. He would take the part of one cautious cat letting the little mouse run free. Someday . . . the chair came down with a bang. Someday he was going to marry Autumn Dale. And what a life they would have. Two redheads plus a couple more redheaded kids — it should be interesting.

It was typical of Dr. McBain that once he left the office, all personal worries and desires were left inside. On the floor he was the usual efficient doctor. Several times Autumn caught herself staring at him, unable to believe the cool machine working alongside her was a man who had declared his love. It was impossible. It also irritated her a little. How could he be so cool, so detached? What a man! Heaven help the woman he married. And yet that little nagging voice inside kept asking, *Would it really be all that bad?*

The October days stayed beautiful. Warmish days, cold nights. It was a riot of color. Gold, red, orange, russet, etched against the solid red-rock mountain at the side of town. There was peace in Dale, a peace they all needed. April was responding beautifully. Every day found her more and more competent. While Dr. McBain still didn't let her give medications or actually assist in surgery, there was much for her to do. She loved it.

And she had learned to care for Autumn, as she had said, as a real sister. Every day brought them closer, and when she'd trot in from the hospital, calling, "I'm home," Autumn and Letty would exchange glances of pure joy. Now and then something came back to April's mind, not as fast as they had hoped, but little things. One had been the result of Dr. McBain's finagling.

"Things are a little quieter now," he said one day. "Why don't you gals take a day off together and go to one of the canyons? I might even be persuaded to join you." His mocking tones hid the wistfulness for a trip with Autumn. He wasn't the type to beg or plead. He was playing the waiting game. In the meantime, a trip would be fun.

April responded first. "Oh, could we?"

But it was Autumn who cast a weather eye

at the hills. "We'd better make it soon if we're going. The tops of those canyons are high elevation and get snow early." She saw April's downcast face and conceded, "Actually, though, this has been such a warm fall, we can still make it."

"How about tomorrow? Dr. Archer and Maxine can hold down the place."

"What canyon do you want to visit this time?" Autumn asked. "Zion? Bryce? Cedar Breaks? Or even the north rim of the Grand Canyon?"

But April's answer surprised her. "Oh, let's go back to Zion! I always liked it best. It's so big, and red, and craggy, and . . ." She caught the stares the other two were giving her.

"I'm remembering! I've been there!" It was the cherry on top of the whipped cream dessert, the final fillip to make their day perfect.

From the stunted cedars along the highway to the blue sky above, everything was just as it should have been. When they reached Zion Canyon, April was almost off the edge of her seat.

"We're almost to the tunnel, what's its name? — Mt. Caramel."

"Mt. Carmel," Autumn corrected. Her palms were moist with excitement. Why hadn't they thought to bring April here sooner?

"Look! There's the entrance!"

But Autumn shook her head. "No, it isn't the entrance. It's only one of the several huge window-like openings for air. You know the tunnel is a long one, blasted through the middle of a solid rock mountain. It was really something to get it built."

They were winding up, up to the entrance to the tunnel. Such a wonderful, interesting place! Giant layers of red and white earth made the mountains look like layer cakes. Huge buttresses of red rock guarded the canyon which ranged from a half mile wide to a mere twenty feet in places.

"Pull in over there." Autumn motioned. The jeep swung into a parking spot. "We'll take a trail. It's a hard climb but worth it. The view of the canyon is one you'll remember."

What an understatement! Never had Matthew McBain felt quite as he did when he reached the last rise of the trail. There were a few faint traces of an early snow on the ground and it was slippery.

"Watch your step!" he called to the girls, buttoning his heavy coat up around his neck.

It was cold, even under the brilliant blue

sky. What must it be like to be up here in a storm? He shuddered at the thought and gazed into the vast space before him. Why hadn't he taken the time to come here before? He didn't want to talk, it was too awe-inspiring.

How could water create such havoc, such depths and shadows? Autumn had said the Virgin River was considered responsible, the tributaries cutting three canyons across the southern Utah plateau, with Zion the largest and most beautiful. Yet as he stood there he found it inconceivable to believe a river had done it.

Without warning April whirled and began running down the trail, back to the jeep. Matt rushed after her, with Autumn close behind. But April was running in flight, in fear. Of what? The other two didn't know. One moment she had been standing there with them, silently enjoying the view. The next she was rushing heedlessly down the trail.

"Thank God there's no snow on the trail." Dr. McBain's words came through clenched teeth. He was gaining on April now, while Autumn fell behind. She had thought she was in good shape from ride-out calls, but not to run down a mountain trail.

It was a long way back to the jeep. When

111

Autumn finally rounded the last bend in the trail, she stood there, transfixed. Her sister was in Dr. McBain's arms, crying her heart out. Cold fear touched Autumn. What was it? What had she remembered to start her off like that, almost as if she were running for her life? She choked down her own feelings and stepped up to them.

"What is it, April?"

It was a long time before she answered. When she did, it was in bits and pieces, like a lovely vase smashed, only shards remaining. "He said we'd come back . . . we didn't."

"Who said you'd come back, April?" Dr. McBain's voice was sharp, demanding.

But April shook her head. "I — I don't know. Someone. Someone who said he loved me. Why didn't we come back? Who is he? Where is he? Why can't I remember?" There was despair in her voice. "If only I could think! I knew I was supposed to meet him. I thought maybe if I came back down here, he'd be here."

Her eyes widened with fear. "But I heard footsteps behind me. Someone was following, just like they followed me in Salt Lake City."

"What!" This time the doctor gave her a hard shake. "Who followed you in Salt Lake City? Why didn't you tell me?"

Even in her concern for April, Autumn noted the proprietary *me* the doctor had used and smiled bitterly. So much for his declaration of love for herself. Evidently it really was April who interested him.

But April's eyes took on a look of remembering. "Why . . . I meant to. But when we got here, you were all so good to me, and kept me so busy, I guess it just seemed like a bad dream. We had all those patients, and then the babies, and she . . ." She shuddered. "It wasn't until today when I heard those footsteps behind me that I remembered. There were footsteps in Salt Lake City. There was someone watching my hotel room, and one night . . ." She looked over her shoulder to see no one else was around. The place was empty except for one lone squirrel sitting on a stone wall, head cocked, eavesdropping on their conversation.

"The night before I left, I heard a board creak outside my room. I rushed to the door and locked it. The knob turned in my hand."

Autumn shook her head. Was she really on top of Zion Canyon listening to her twin sister tell such a fantastic story? Yes, the squirrel was still there and the red-rock walls. She was awake. This was no nightmare.

"I waited. I don't think I even breathed. Then steps went away. I looked out my window and he was there, the man in the dark coat who had been there before. I couldn't stay there worrying all night. I checked out, had a taxi called for the back entrance, and crept downstairs. The taxi driver took me to the hospital, and Mrs. Duffy found an empty room for me to stay in. I came to Dale the next day."

Autumn and Dr. McBain exchanged puzzled glances over her head. Who could have been following her? An old friend? It didn't make sense. No one knew April had been a victim of amnesia. Anyone who recognized her would have approached her, not skulked around the hotel where she lived.

"I don't like this. I don't like this at all," Autumn said.

But April had regained some of her composure. She sat up and dried her eyes. "It's all over now. It's just that when I heard those footsteps on the trail . . ." She began to laugh. "They were *your* footsteps, weren't they?"

It eased the tension. But on the way home, Autumn was very quiet, so much so April finally accused, "Look, you aren't worrying about that man, are you? It's all over. Nothing has happened since I left Salt Lake

City. I'm free, here, and I love it!" She threw her arms wide as if to embrace the whole scene they were leaving.

If only it is all over. But I don't believe it. Whoever was interested enough to follow her in Salt Lake City could have ways and means to find out where she is. But who? Why? Autumn's thoughts were racing like a squirrel in a cage. Even the good dinner at a nearby steakhouse failed to cheer her. She had too much to think over. She didn't want to alarm April and yet, suppose there was still a danger, some unknown threat of some kind hanging over her sister?

"We're home, Autumn."

Autumn had lost track of the miles. The day which had started so promising had ended for her in worry and fear. There was a growing suspicion inside her, a gnawing doubt. It seemed impossible, too iffy to be real, and yet . . .

"April." She deliberately kept her voice casual, but Dr. McBain caught the carefully hidden anxiety. "Do you have any idea whatsoever of who might have been following you?"

They had come into the living room at home. Dr. McBain was bringing in the picnic basket which had been discarded in favor of a hot meal. To their surprise April nodded.

"I suppose it's crazy, but there was someone . . ." Her voice trailed off, then steadied. "As I say, it may be crazy. But when I was at the hospital a man came in for an appendectomy. I took a call from his room. He called me April. It surprised me, although I suppose he might have heard one of the nurses call me that. He was really strange. He was nasty when I said he couldn't have dinner because of his surgery the next morning. He even threatened me."

She brushed her hand across her eyes. "I told Mrs. Duffy I was afraid of him, but I didn't know why." She paused.

"Did you see him again?" Autumn asked.

"No. He was transferred to another area. But it was after he was discharged that I was followed. I wondered if he'd been so upset about the incident in the hospital he was trying to scare me or something." April smothered a yawn and started for the door.

"April, do you happen to remember the patient's name?"

She shook her head. "No, wait. It was a funny name, not too common. Oh, I know what it was. His name was Quint Reed." This time she yawned out loud and laughed. "I'd better get to bed before I fall asleep."

In a moment she had gone. Dr. McBain turned to Autumn.

"What do you . . . Autumn!"

The girl's face was pale as snow, her hands clenched until the knuckles showed white.

"Autumn, what's wrong?"

She tried twice before she could get the words out of her parched throat. "That man — Quint Reed — he was the man who tried to make love to me, the man April had planned to marry until she found out what he really was, the man she ordered out and told she never wanted to see him again!"

Chapter 8

"*What!*" Dr. McBain's word cracked like a pistol shot.

Autumn didn't even hear it. "Then he will know where April is!" she said. "He knows this country as well as we do. He lived in Kanab for years. He took April to all the canyons when they were dating. She loved them." Her voice was toneless. Then with a rush of pain she cried out, "What can we do? She's been through enough! What if he comes here? He's bound to come sooner or later."

A slight smile crossed Matthew McBain's face, a very unpleasant smile. "I think, my dear, I would be glad to have him come."

For the first time Autumn saw beneath the cool doctor's skin to the tremendous strength underneath. It confirmed her own earlier feelings. *I'm glad I decided it had to be this way. No man on earth can harm April if she belongs to Dr. McBain.*

"Do you think we should warn April?" Autumn asked.

Dr. McBain shook his head. "If we do, we'll have to go into the reasons why. She's coming along very slowly, but without having to face too many painful memories all at once. I hesitate to shock her into trying to remember everything."

"You're right, of course. She's going to have to face the whole sending Quint Reed away, then the death of our parents. But it's going to be so hard not to even give her a hint!"

Dr. McBain considered for a moment. "We really don't have to warn her about Quint Reed, Autumn. She already distrusted and feared him from their hospital encounter even before she came here."

"I can't understand how he could just happen to be on her ward at the exact time she was there!"

The doctor shook his head. "Those things do happen. Just as I came here soon after meeting her and helping her find a job. If you hadn't needed more nurses, I probably wouldn't have thought to ask her to come here."

Autumn's heart gave a great leap. It didn't sound as if he were in love with April after that last sentence. But she steeled herself.

He could be easily enough. When April got back her memory, she'd be the most charming girl alive.

When Dr. McBain had gone, Autumn still sat on the couch staring at the wall. Maybe she should go away. If she did, April and the doctor would be free to work together and fall in love. She herself would be away from the pain of seeing the doctor daily and not letting him know she cared. And how she cared! She had never thought love could strike this fast but expected it would be a growing thing. In one way it had grown. Yet she knew there had been an attraction for her from the time the big, confident, red-headed doctor arrived.

If I go away it might solve everything. But would it? Dr. McBain could watch April on duty, but what about when she was home? Letty was on night duty. She'd be no help if Quint Reed came to Dale. There were no homes close enough that April would be protected, and they had decided not to tell her she even needed protection.

I can't go. I'll have to stay here and make the best of it. One of Autumn's qualities was once she made a decision, she never looked back. Right or wrong she would live with it at least until circumstances changed the need for that decision. Sometimes it was all she could do to carry on, but she always said, "I'd rather make a wrong decision and have to live with it than make no decision at all. My worries always come until I've made the decision. After that I don't waste time looking back, picking it to pieces, and wondering if I should have done differently."

Perhaps it was this trait which helped her through the winter months in Dale. Time and again she gritted her teeth and deliberately looked away from Matthew McBain's eyes to keep from betraying herself. She could see that her coolness was doing the trick. No longer did he allow his feelings to show. She was convincing him — or was she? Once in a while she did catch a biding-my-time look, but she ignored it. The pain inside had subsided, especially because of April's progress.

And April was making progress. Just before Christmas there had been a major breakthrough. Dr. McBain had taken the two sisters in the jeep to get a Christmas tree. It was when they returned, snow-covered, triumphant, bearing the most beautiful tree they could find, that it happened.

"It's too bad we'll be alone for Christmas," April said.

They were seated in the living room, floor

protected with newspapers, having a cup of hot cider before getting the tree ready for decorating.

Autumn glanced at April. "We won't be alone. You know Letty will be here, and Dr. Archer and Dr. McBain. Even Maxine and Sancho are coming."

April stared into the fire. The thin cheeks had filled out and were now rosy. "Yes, I know. But it isn't quite the same." She shot an apologetic look at Dr. McBain. "Dad and Mom always loved Christmas so." Tears filled the blue eyes. "This is my first Christmas without them."

Autumn felt frozen to her chair, but Dr. McBain asked, very softly, "What happened to your parents, April?"

"They were killed in a plane crash. I saw it in the paper and heard it on TV. I ran from my apartment. Maybe I could get to the hospital before they died. I had to see them, just once more! It was a miserable day. Just before I got to the hospital I slipped, fell . . ." Her voice faltered, but Dr. McBain picked up the story.

"And you were brought to our hospital."

"Yes." The blue eyes were questioning now. "I was in such a hurry I didn't even take my purse."

Autumn remembered Dr. McBain's first

description of April when she had come to the hospital:

"She had no purse, no identifying marks of any kind. . . . We found a large lump on her head. Somehow she must have fallen, or even been struck . . ." It was a crucial moment.

"I remember my apartment! I can go there, get my clothes, find out who I really am!"

The joy in April's face tightened Autumn's throat. While her twin had remembered their parents, she evidently had not remembered her sister. Was the memory of Autumn fighting Quint Reed's advances so painful she simply *couldn't* remember? The thought choked off Autumn's breath, but Dr. McBain had taken April's hands in his.

"April, I'd like to ask you to do something, the hardest thing you've ever had to do."

The girl looked at him in surprise. Even Autumn didn't know what was coming.

"April, I want you to take me to Salt Lake City and to your apartment. I want Autumn to go with us. She'll help you pack your clothes. But, April" — his steady gaze held her own — "I don't want you to find out who you are — not that way!"

She jerked away from him, standing up.

Her hand went to her mouth, but it couldn't keep back the words.

"You don't *want* me to find out who I am?"

Autumn started to speak, to defend her twin, but Dr. McBain's look impaled her, caused her to lean back in her chair. Vaguely she began to understand.

Not so April. "I would do anything for you, Dr. McBain, anything — but not this, not this!" Her voice had risen to a shrill cry. "I have to know. I can't go on living in this half world!"

His emerald gaze never wavered from the cry of anguish. If anything it only became more fixed. "April, you have made progress since you came here. There is only one thing left for you to find out — who you actually are. Can't you trust me?"

For a moment her defiance kept her standing. Then she lost some of it and sat back down. She was by no means beaten, but at least she would listen.

"Would you tell me why?" A sudden suspicion narrowed her eyes. "You know who I am, don't you?"

"Yes. So does Autumn."

April's eyes sought out those of the girl she had called her sister, pleading for reassurance.

"It's all right. April. It is *all right.*"

Slowly the tension went out of April. She gave a long sigh, almost a sob. And she turned to the doctor. "Then I'll do what you ask."

Dr. McBain's knuckles which had been white from his grasp on the chair arms relaxed. With sudden compassion he told April, "It will only be for a little while. But you will be far better off to let it come naturally."

Was it the nursing training April had before the accident which gave her the knowledge that what he said was true? She nodded slowly, but asked another question.

"It isn't because I've done anything terrible, is it?"

Dr. McBain laughed clear from the toes. "Not at all. We just want you to come back at your own speed and not be forced."

But the girl opposite him had still one more question. "Is my name really April?" There was far more anxiety in her voice than there should have been.

The doctor was congratulating himself on her giving in and didn't notice. But Autumn did. Autumn, the twin whose heart was bursting to be recognized. "Your name is really April."

Strangely enough it seemed to reassure

the girl. "Then we're still April and Autumn."

This time the doctor did notice. He hastened to add, "Yes, you are. April and Autumn — alike yet different. But both wonderful girls." To cover the huskiness in his throat, he jumped up, heedless of the snow melting all over the place from his wet boots.

"Hey, get back on the newspapers!" Autumn was close to tears. She grabbed a broom, pretending to chase the big doctor across the room. It was enough to cause Letty, who had stepped to the doorway to see what was causing all the commotion, to peer down over her glasses.

"My land, what's going on in here?"

Dr. McBain grabbed her and danced her around, then took the broom from Autumn and swept up the mess. But before he left, it was decided to go for April's things the next day.

Because of the holiday the hospital workload was light. Letty, Maxine, and Dr. Archer would handle it. The girls would stay in April's apartment, then settle with the owner.

April's face had been drawn with worry. "I know my things will be there because it's on the top of a private house. What must

Mrs. Grady think? She liked me and was so good to me. All these months and not knowing what happened!"

Mrs. Grady proved to be all April had said. White-haired, kindly, she had left the room just as it was when "Mary Johnson," as April had called herself, left it.

"I knew she'd come back! I knew she wouldn't go off and leave everything," Mrs. Grady said. "But when I called the police, they couldn't find a trace of her, and I hated to push it." Now tears streamed down the good woman's face.

"Will you be all alone now?" Autumn asked.

But Mrs. Grady shook her head. "My grandson's been wanting to come stay with me. But I wouldn't let him have Mary's room until I knew for sure she wouldn't be back."

It was a strange night spent in the twin beds upstairs. Both April and Autumn were filled with their own thoughts. Earlier they had packed, April conscientiously letting Autumn pick up any papers, her purse, checkbook, and so forth, that might give away her real identity. Autumn could see it was hard for her. She almost wanted to tell April the whole story, but she was under the doctor's orders to be silent.

"She has to come back her own way and in her own time. You saw how she reacted when she remembered your parents' deaths. If she remembers all the rest, she may not be able to handle it."

Reluctantly Autumn agreed. But after a few hours' fitful sleep she woke to hear April crying softly. Slipping from bed she went across the room shivering against the cold December night.

Wordlessly April clung to her, giving way to grief for her lost mother and father, grief Autumn had experienced many months ago, but which had been denied April because of her amnesia. After a long time she quieted and fell asleep. Autumn crawled back in bed realizing Dr. McBain had been right. April was in no condition now to accept the rest of her story. She was still a patient, and would be until her strength was regained and she could handle it.

What a wonderful thing the human organism is, Autumn marveled. It wasn't the first time she had felt that way. Wide awake now, she relived events from her nursing career, so many of them! When had she first learned respect for the body and its natural healing processes? The first time she had watched a child recover from surgery? Or the time she had assisted at her first bone-setting, then been assigned to special the patient, seeing how that same bone knit beautifully?

I could never be anything in the world except a nurse. Even when I marry I will never give it up. Maybe I won't work full-time, but I have to share my skills with those who need me. Gradually the lashes became lower on Autumn's cheeks until at last she slept. But her last waking thought was how wise Dr. McBain had been. April's mind would not allow her to recall traumatic events until she was strong enough to stand them.

Christmas flashed by in a whirl of snow, packages, and good food. January followed, cold, bitter. February gave some promise of better days, March added to it, and then came April. With the coming of her birth month, April Dale blossomed. The winter days had held no dread for her as they had for Dr. McBain and Autumn, who knew that with spring Quint Reed would surely appear on the scene.

"I'll almost welcome his coming," Dr. McBain told Autumn one day. "I hate this waiting, not knowing where he is. You know I asked the hospital staff in Salt Lake to keep an eye out for him, but he hasn't been around. I couldn't put the police on his trail. Being a creep and standing outside a hotel

129

aren't enough to convict a man, unfortunately!"

"I know." While spring had caused April to bloom, Autumn looked like a little wilted flower. There was a shadow in her eyes now, something always present. If April had not been so gloriously happy, she couldn't have missed it. Dr. McBain saw it and his heart ached. He knew the fight Autumn was making. He knew without asking the sleepless nights the girl, who had become a woman in front of his very eyes, was experiencing. He even suspected the reason. If and when April remembered her former love for Quint Reed, would she also remember Autumn's innocence in the man's betrayal? Or would she blame Autumn?

The onslaught of chicken pox in Dale was almost a relief. The winter months had been slow around the hospital. Not now! Day after day they came, mothers with children who had chicken pox. Light cases and heavy. Advanced and beginning. Sometimes Autumn thought if she saw one more chicken pox case she'd turn around and walk out. But she never did. She doled out cream for the itching sores and gave out prescriptions scribbled by a tired Dr. McBain.

It was especially hard on the larger families. One child would get it, then in ten days or two weeks, another would.

Autumn brushed a weary hand over her face. "I've made so many ride-out calls I'm getting saddle sore!"

Dr. McBain was very still, then he spoke slowly. "You will never know how much I appreciate all this. I have seen nurses in city hospitals work long hours during an emergency. I have seen incredible feats of strength when strength was gone. But I have never seen anything like the way you gals have kept going, all of you. Letty, Maxine, April, you. If I had had any regrets about coming to Dale instead of staying with a larger hospital, this epidemic, and we can call it that, would have shouted them down forever."

It was a long speech for the usually terse doctor. It touched Autumn. She was so tired of fighting, fighting the chicken pox, the fear of what spring would bring, her own love for the doctor. But she couldn't weaken now. She had seen the fondness creeping into Dr. McBain's eyes for the "new" April. In time he would forget her and concentrate on April — she hoped.

If she could have looked inside Dr. McBain's head at that exact minute, she would have alternated between despair and joy. Yes, he had grown fond of April, but the way he would have loved a younger sister if he'd had one. She seemed so much younger than her twin. Was it because of her memory lapse? At times she was like a child in her approach to things. Whatever the reason, Autumn seemed years older. April was a child to be protected, Autumn was a woman to be cherished.

Of them all, April weathered the chicken pox best. She was tireless. She seemed to thrive on being needed. Besides, April had a secret. It began in a small way. One Sunday evening Letty asked the girls to attend a special worship service at the community church. Autumn was too tired, but April went with Letty. After the service, there were general introductions. Letty and Autumn had worried about this, but April had changed so much even the townspeople didn't recognize her. Letty made sure not to use the name April except to newcomers.

There was one newcomer, Jason Wells, who hadn't taken his eyes off April from the time she walked in the door. Jason Wells had been gone from Dale for several years. He was oldest of the Wells family who had just welcomed baby daughter Faith into their midst.

He always laughed, "You know Mom. As

soon as one of us got old enough so she thought she was going to be left lonesome, she'd go and have another baby!"

Annie agreed. "I like to space them out."

They were spaced out, all right! Jason was in his mid-twenties. He had graduated from college with honors, majoring in geology. Now he was on an assignment back in Dale.

He stared at April, wondering. Somewhere back in his memory he had seen blue eyes like that. But it was too far back in the past. He had left Dale even before high-school days to get a good, solid prep-school background for his college work. Now he was impressed with the dainty girl, her brown hair and blue eyes, her simple skirt and blouse.

When he met her, it clicked. The name "April." A day long ago he had been in the hospital to have a cut stitched. There had been a blue-eyed girl, one of the Dale twins.

"Aren't you . . ." Suddenly Jason saw Letty violently shaking her head at him from behind April. He didn't understand her signals but had enough respect for her to substitute, "Aren't you one of the nurses who helped take care of my mom when she had Faith?"

April's face lit up. "Oh, Yes! How are they?"

133

It took all the way from the church home for the enterprising Jason Wells to tell her, and not before he'd asked her out to dinner her next day off. But after April told him good night and slipped into the house, Letty was waiting for him. She knew Jason had recognized April. Leading him to a bench out of sight from the house, she explained in a few quick words.

"You mean she remembers some things but not others?"

Letty nodded. "Dr. McBain doesn't want her forced or pushed in any way."

Jason agreed. "He's right. I won't do anything to let her know I suspect anything." He paused. "But it is all right to ask her out, isn't it?"

Letty only smiled. As far as she was concerned, it was more than all right.

Chapter 9

It had been a long winter for a man named Quint Reed. He had followed his original plan and arrived in Kanab from Salt Lake City shortly after April was picked up by Dr. McBain. He was wise enough to know he should keep out of sight as much as possible, so his furtive trips to Dale went unnoticed, as he had planned.

He came and went at odd hours, finding out all kinds of interesting information. April was working at the hospital. April was living with Autumn in the big house once more. Evidently she didn't even know it was her own room in which she lived. Some of the conversations he heard while crouched under windowsills told him that. His smile was evil. She'd remember him, he'd see to that!

During the long winter months the man was busy, very busy. His first idea for both revenge and pleasure had expanded. Now he chuckled as he set about preparing a cover for what lay ahead. He let his hair grow. He let his beard grow. It was a vastly changed man who appeared infrequently in Kanab for supplies. Although the day of the desert-rat-type prospector was nearly over, still once in a while one would come through. This is exactly what Quint Reed counted on. A few hints here and there, a well-purchased gold pan, an outfit. Then he disappeared for several weeks.

Yet those winter months were not idle months. In spite of the weather, the floor of the canyons was pretty well protected from too much snowfall, often because of the huge rock overhangs. Patiently, carefully, watching detail, Quint Reed traced his way to a rotting cabin hidden so far back in the rocks it seemed impossible anyone could ever have built it.

Was it an outlaw stronghold from a more lawless day? Or just the cabin of an old prospector, with his desire for gold? Whatever it was, Quint knew it. His had been no idle boast about knowing the canyons, and knowing them well. Bit by bit he put the cabin into a little more livable shape.

"Got to have it nice for my girl friend!" he told a curious bird nearby. Then he laughed, but it was not pleasant to hear. Somehow

April ordering him out that day so long ago had warped his brain. He had been counting on the Dale fortune. Even if he had married April, he wouldn't have been true to her — but so what? She wouldn't have had to know everything he did. Besides, she was pretty.

If only he hadn't made a pass at Autumn that day! He should have known she would resist any advances from him, she'd never liked him. But his supreme self-confidence coupled with the archaic idea that women liked caveman stuff wouldn't allow him to think any woman would resist. Many times he had cursed the fate that had brought April in just then. Well, that was past. Now he would set himself up to get what he wanted.

One thing Quint Reed wouldn't admit. In the past months it was no longer so easy to find a charming woman. Had the Dale twins jinxed him? In the dark winter hours he thought of the times with April — her laughter, her trust in him. Perhaps memory blew it all out of proportion, but by the time spring came, Quint had convinced himself he really was in love with April.

Everything would work out fine. He'd get her out here to his cabin and keep her until she agreed to marry him. It never once occurred to him he was thinking like something out of an Old West story. He merely saw what he wanted to see. Either she'd fall in love with him again or he'd marry her anyway. After being off in the canyons with him for a time, she'd have to. She wasn't one of these new-fangled women who didn't care what people thought.

He smiled again, eyes narrowed to a slit. Her very amnesia would play in his favor, that and his beard and long hair. She wouldn't even know who he really was until he chose to tell her.

So as winter winds gave way to spring breezes he prepared and waited, in his arrogance, secure that his plan would work. April would marry him. It would solve all his problems, financial, emotional, everything. He had decided to wait until early summer. It would be the best time for his little jaunt to Dale alone — although his return journey would not be alone. Sometimes his heart beat so rapidly it nearly choked him. Just a few more months, and then . . . success!

Quint Reed wasn't the only one waiting for summer. Everyone at Big Rock General was also waiting, for different reasons. Dr. McBain would take a few weeks off to go back to Salt Lake City. There was a special surgeon's conference with an old friend in charge. He wanted to be there. The chicken pox had finally subsided. Now if only things would stay quiet for a while. He had unsuccessfully tried to get April to go back and visit, but she was determined not to leave Dale.

"I love it here too much!" She certainly looked as if she did.

Was it only Dale she loved? But the doctor was too preoccupied to notice. Not Autumn. She saw the radiant glow on her twin's face. It was the same look of love she felt in her own heart but didn't dare let show. It was the look April had worn for Quint Reed long ago, but with a difference. That had been wild excitement; this new look included contentment that had not been there before. April had never been more beautiful than with the coming spring.

It's really true — we reflect our seasons, Autumn thought, watching her sister. *April glows in the springtime. I come alive in the fall.* Suddenly she wished passionately that summer was over, that long waiting time full of fear that Quint Reed would appear. With fall leading into winter she would feel safe again.

There were times when the burden of her sister's safety and mental health was almost too much to bear. The strain of never knowing. Autumn would almost welcome an incident. At least then it would be in the open. Now she didn't breathe a sigh of relief until the doors were locked at night and April was asleep.

The worry left marks. Finally, even April in her happiness noticed and spoke to the doctor about it.

"Something's bothering Autumn. Do you know what it is?"

He looked at her seriously. "Yes, but it's nothing that can be helped. Not now." He sighed.

April could see it bothered him, too. "Can't I do anything, just anything?"

He looked into her eager, upturned face, comparing it with the pale face he had first seen just a year before. "Yes, there is. You can get her outdoors more. Sunshine and good air will help her. Tell her you want to take some of the ride-out calls for routine treatments, injections, and so on. She'll go with you."

"Thanks, Doctor, you're a dear!" April skipped away, face bright.

All Autumn heard was the "dear." She had stepped up to ask him about a treatment. Her heart fell like lead. So it really was true. April was in love with Matthew McBain.

It's what you wanted, she reminded herself savagely, but it didn't help much. For an instant she thought of how Jason Wells had been taking April places, how she had hoped that maybe — but it didn't sound that way now. Autumn's voice was colorless as she inquired about the patient.

"Mr. Jarvis is asking if he can have something for the pain." He was an elderly man who had fallen and broken his hip. For one of his years he was doing amazingly well. Things were healing rapidly. But there were times when he had intense pain.

"Yes, give him one of those tablets I prescribed. But not any oftener than every four hours."

A wan smile crossed Autumn's face. "He won't need them that often. He didn't even ask for this one until it was pretty bad."

Matt watched her walk away, noticing how the uniform hung on her slim figure. She had lost weight that winter. Things couldn't go on as they now were. He spread his hands helplessly. It didn't do any good to reassure her of his love. He had tried to bring it up again, but she only shook her head, indicating unwillingness to discuss it.

Would things with April ever settle down? He hoped so. Even though he had told Autumn he wouldn't push her, it was hard seeing her every day, dreaming every night of what life with her could be.

The only really happy ones were April and Jason Wells. More and more he sought out her company. She was alarmed at her rapid response. Love should take longer, not come with a pounce! But the look in Jason's eyes told April he felt the same way. They picnicked, drove, even found a tiny stream dammed up by winter debris for swimming. More and more April had the feeling this was no stranger but part of her life from the beginning of time.

The day came when they were seated under a stunted tree on the way home from Bryce Canyon. Again April had remembered being there before, the lacy pink and cream formations that differed so much from Zion Canyon. On the way home she was strangely quiet. June had come to the canyon country and it was warm. Unseasonable rains had brought out a late crop of tiny desert flowers.

"Shall we stop and look at them?" Jason caught her nod and pulled the car off the road, then helped her out. Before them lay the tiny flowers that were almost like a carpet.

"It's a miracle the way those dry seeds lie there practically forever, then burst into bloom after a good rain!" she said.

But Jason wasn't looking at the flowers. Suddenly he felt the time had come. He reached for April's hand.

"It's a miracle after being away from Dale all these years to come home — and find you."

April looked at him sharply, but she didn't pull away. The next minute he had her in his arms. His first kiss stirred her deeply and she clung to him. When he released her, she looked up to him, but her question was not what he would have expected.

"Jason, did I know you . . . before?"

He knew instantly he could not lie to her. "Yes, April. A long time ago."

She was quiet, looking across the desert. "There are times when I feel as if I lived in Dale, as if I know it well. Jason, the name Dale, it rings a bell, it has from the time Dr. McBain asked me to come here. Is it possible, that is, am I related to the Dales in some way?"

He held his breath, but forced himself to meet her eyes squarely. "Yes, you could say that you are."

As suddenly as her questions started they ceased. Finally, she spoke again. "Then Autumn is really part of me." She caught his surprise. "I've felt from the first she knew more about me than she was telling. Then at Christmastime Dr. McBain said they both knew who I am." She smiled, her hand gripping his. "I'm getting it all back."

It was too much for him. "And when you do, April? What then?"

"Why, I suppose I'll stay right here in Dale and marry and have kids and work at Big Rock Hospital and . . ."

His heart was thumping. "How does Mrs. April Wells sound?" Before she could pull back, he kissed her again then pulled her to her feet.

"I'm not asking for any promises. You still have things to remember. Just remember, along with all those other things, when you go looking for that husband and kids, Jason Wells has his application in first!"

If at that moment he had asked, April would have agreed to follow him to the end of the earth. His strength, his tenderness and understanding, were everything she'd never had when she was engaged before. Jason didn't see the paleness that crept over her face at the thought. For the first time she was starting to remember. She had been engaged, something had happened, what was it? But the memory was gone before it took hold, leaving her weak.

Jason's grip on the steering wheel was indicative of his grip on himself. He was glad, so glad he had told April what he did. He had seen the joy in her face, had even suspected she would have said yes if he had pushed it. But he wouldn't. It wasn't fair to her until she was clear on everything else in her mind. He had no way of knowing April's feeling of security — her knowledge of his love, although he hadn't put it in those exact words — would be the key to unlocking that final door in her mind. The unconscious dread of facing that last shattering scene with Autumn and Quint would be removed simply because April had a new love, someone who cared.

"Are — are you planning to stay in Dale? I thought you were a geologist."

He hid his grin at her hesitancy, the color in her face.

"Yes. I am. I'll finish this project this summer, but since I came back I realized I have roots here. My family, the people, all this." He gestured toward the little town of Dale nestling under the big red mountain. "I like it here. Besides, the new high school principal has approached me about starting a new program in geology for the students. I have my teacher's credentials as well as majoring in geology. I think I'd like to try teaching for a while."

April stared. My goodness, he certainly sounded all set. His face was innocent, but she was still suspicious.

"I see. And just when did you make all these plans?"

His look at her was bland, almost daring her to make an issue of it. "Oh, the first Monday I was home I talked with the principal. Ever since then I've been pretty sure what I was going to do."

"The first Monday? And Monday comes after Sunday night, doesn't it? And Sunday night is church at the community church, isn't it?"

His eyes rounded, as if it were a new thought. "Why, so it is."

They both laughed, sheer joy at being together. But as the desert-tanned strong fingers left the steering wheel to capture the little hand that was just now starting to tan, April slid closer to him. She felt as if she had come home, where she belonged. His goodnight kiss was tender, not demanding, just loving. She leaned against the door, filled with happiness. How could she ever live up to such a wonderful man as Jason Wells?

She didn't know, couldn't guess, that the oldest of the Wells boys was even then asking himself, *What have I ever done to deserve a girl like April?*

The miles between Dale and the Wells ranch flashed by, as did the turnoff! It wasn't until Jason was a good two miles on down the road that he realized he should have turned into home long before. But the sheepish grin didn't even try to cover the fact he didn't care one bit. It had just been that much longer to think of April and their future.

If only Autumn could have eavesdropped on that little conversation! It would have saved heartache, especially a few days later when April wandered into her room just at bedtime and curled up on the bed.

"Autumn, have you ever been in love?"

Autumn's heart nearly stopped. Why was she asking? Had she discovered something? She had been brushing her hair so it didn't seem forced to swing it forward and cover her face. It did muffle her words a bit. "Of course."

A frown crossed April's face. "Why do you say it that way?"

"Because every red-blooded American girl who is twenty-one years old has probably been in love or thought she was at some time."

Her answers weren't very helpful, but April tried again. "How did you know? Was he the right man?" April didn't know what she was putting Autumn through with her questions.

"Oh, they always say you'll know when you're in love." Autumn ignored the second question, but April persisted.

"Was he the right man?"

"I'm still single, aren't I?"

April laughed, then sank back against the pillow. "Autumn, I'm in love."

Here it came, what Autumn had prayed for, dreaded, and anticipated with both relief and fear. All she could do was clutch her hairbrush and get out weakly, "Oh?"

April didn't even notice the tiny response. "He's tall and strong. When I am with him I feel as if nothing in the world could hurt me. We can do a great deal of good here."

The pain inside Autumn didn't blot out April's words. Through its haze the twin who didn't know she was a twin went on.

"He won't ask me to marry him until I've remembered everything. I know now that once I was engaged and something happened. It must not have been the right man. I can see that. I can't imagine anyone else in the whole world being the right man for me!"

So it was settled. April would marry Dr. McBain as soon as she recovered completely. On impulse, Autumn swung around to cry out something, warning April to be sure, but the radiance of April's face stopped her. She had found what she wanted from life, nothing else would do. The words died on Autumn's lips. Some of her own pain also died.

For a moment she saw into her twin sister's heart, a glimpse that was almost sacred. Even among twins it is not often such a look can be given. Over her own rush of feeling Autumn triumphed. At that moment a verse from the Bible crossed her mind.

Greater love hath no man than this, that he lay down his life for a friend.

April slipped out unheeded, to hug her joy. But Autumn sat on the bed, at least for the moment free of her own longings. She wasn't laying down her life for a friend, but she was giving up her own life for her sister. Vaguely she wondered why it didn't hurt more. Was it because of that one look she had been given into April's heart? Nurses saw more than most people, yet this was something different from anything a patient had ever revealed.

Please, let me be able to keep this feeling. It helps. In the June moonlight, Autumn, a girl who had long ago turned woman, knelt looking out into a garden, and over to a big red-rock mountain at the edge of town.

For at least those moments Autumn had found the most precious gift of all — peace. Her sleep was deep and untroubled. All the tomorrows might dissipate the joy of sacrifice. For tonight, it was enough to be thankful for the strength that had been granted when she most needed it.

Chapter 10

D-Day had arrived, D for Departure, for Dr. McBain, who was off to his conference. The staff of Big Rock Hospital had told him to have a good time and waved him off. He turned his car north toward Salt Lake City, rounded the bend out of town, and was gone.

Autumn watched him go from behind a curtain in one of the wards. There was a strange sinking feeling in her heart. She had come to rely on his strength so much, and now he was gone, leaving her totally responsible for April's safety.

Autumn thought of Dr. McBain's face as he said good-bye. "Take care of April." He checked to see no one else was around. "There's no reason to think this Quint Reed will show up in the few days I'm gone, but to be extra sure, don't let April out alone on calls, even the shortest one."

Autumn's eyes were steady. "I'll take care of her for you."

Matt McBain looked kind of strange. "For me? Oh, sure. For all of us."

But long after he was gone, Autumn thought of his unusual answer. He and April were the same as engaged, weren't they? Why should he find it odd for her to comment as she had? But there was no time for standing around just thinking. She turned to the desk checking the calls that had come in. Pretty routine. Annie Wells would like someone to stop by if they had time, nothing serious, but Faith had a slight cold and the men were so busy it was hard to get into town just then.

Two routine injections just down the street. The hospital patients ranged from a broken arm to a mother-in-waiting, but she wouldn't be due at least until the next day. Letty and Maxine were both helping out and Dr. Archer had promised to stay fairly close to the hospital.

Autumn turned from the desk. Why not get April and ride out to the Wells place? She smiled bitterly. April would love that! In spite of her evident love for the doctor, April was still seeing a lot of Jason Wells. Autumn had mentioned it once.

"Aren't you spending a lot of time with Jason?" She had been unprepared for the high flags of color in April's face.

"Any reason why I shouldn't?"

It had been on the tip of Autumn's tongue to retort, "Well, for a practically engaged girl it seems funny!" but she held it back. It wasn't up to her to point out something April should know.

So April continued to ride and walk with Jason. Autumn couldn't see that Dr. McBain cared. At least if he did, it was well hidden. He came to see the girls when he was free, enjoying Letty's cooking, content to curl up and just rest. He seldom made an effort to be alone with April.

Autumn couldn't figure it out, especially when she had unexpectedly caught the look in his eyes directed toward her once when he had been sitting in a chair. Or had she imagined the tenderness, the longing? Since that night she had made a special effort to keep even tighter reins on her feelings, turning herself into practically an automaton.

"April, let's get this call out to the Wellses done." She couldn't help but note the eagerness in her sister's face, the lighting up, the sparkle in her eyes. Autumn was ashamed of the resentment that went through her. Wasn't it enough for her to have Matthew McBain without trying to snare Jason Wells?

April was thrilled. "Why don't we take

horses this time, instead of the jeep? Then if anything else comes in while we're gone, Dr. Archer and Letty and Maxine can have the jeep."

"That's a good idea. Maxine is excellent on a horse, but Dr. Archer and Letty said they had had it trying to ride those four-legged beasts. Either they use the jeep or we go!"

April laughed. "I know. Letty told me she had ridden horses for enough years. Now it was our turn."

The road was hot and dusty, but both girls were used to it. They wore Mexican-type sombreros which shaded their faces. As they took the turnoff to the Wells place, Autumn was pleased to note how well April had learned to handle her horse. Actually, she had relearned. Before the accident, April had been an expert horsewoman, as was Autumn herself. They had ridden almost before they learned to walk, high on horses in front of their parents.

I wish my parents were here to see April now. Autumn's heart was filled with pride. The pale, troubled girl who had come back to Dale the fall before was gone forever. In her place was a strong, healthy, rosy-cheeked woman with a grand future.

"Hi, Jason!"

Autumn's sharp eyes caught every blush and reflected pleasure in their meeting at the gate. Jason had just ridden in and was still on horseback.

April would have lingered, but with a glance after Autumn, contented herself to whisper, "It's good to see you." And she slipped from her horse and into the house.

Autumn had already washed her hands and was holding Faith, expertly examining the tiny child. "You were right, nothing more than a good old-fashioned summer cold." She rummaged in her medical kit, bringing out the decongestant Dr. Archer had sent in case it was a cold. "Give her this every four hours. It will break things up and she'll be fine. Lots of water and keep her covered but only lightly."

Even as Autumn gave the directions, she laughed. "After all your children, you could probably quote all this better than I can!"

Annie Wells agreed. "Yes, one and all went through the same things. At least the little one escaped chicken pox — this time!"

"I was glad to hear that, too. She's still pretty young. But probably the next go-round she'll have it and get it over with."

"They all do, I suppose."

"Why don't you stay for supper?" Jason asked, his eyes on April. "It's going to be a beautiful evening, and I'll ride home with you."

"Can we, Autumn?"

Even Annie Wells caught the pleading look on April's face. A pleased smile crossed her own face, but she tried not to show it. So that was the way things were! Good! She'd wondered what had suddenly caused Jason to decide to stay and teach in Dale. She also knew who April was, but suspected the truth — the girl didn't remember something.

But Annie Wells wasn't one to pry into other folks' business. She had watched April turn from the washed-out creature she'd been last fall to what she was now. Yes, she'd make a fine daughter-in-law.

"Call the hospital, Autumn," Annie Wells urged. "If there isn't anything pressing, we'd love to have you stay. Besides, I just happened to have killed a couple of young fryers, and of course there's strawberry shortcake and fresh peas and lettuce and —"

Autumn held up her hands. "I give up! How could I resist all that?" She dialed Big Rock Hospital.

"Maxine? Everything okay? The Wellses have asked us to stay for supper . . . You're sure? All right. We'll be back early — around nine. I can take night shift and you and Letty can rest . . . April? Oh, sure, she's fine." Seeing the delighted look April cast at Jason, Autumn added to herself, *She's fine, all right, she's downright satisfied, looks like a cat with a canary feather in her mouth!*

"Why does everyone keep asking how I am?" April asked as they all did justice to the delicious meal. "I feel — I feel as if I'm under surveillance or something!" April's protest was drowned by Jason's voice, more earnest than he'd intended.

"Maybe because you're so special to — to all of us," he added, but it was a lame effort.

This time even Mr. Wells and the two older boys noticed.

"Jason's got a girl friend, Jason's got a girl friend!" The fifteen-year-old's taunt brought color to April's face, but Mrs. Wells intervened.

"I think we're ready for our shortcake." The advent of the three-layer, split hot-biscuit shortcake loaded with berries and topped with whipped cream successfully diverted any more teasing. But Autumn didn't forget it. Really, how could April! She hadn't even denied it. Suddenly the delicious dessert tasted like sawdust, and when they got ready to go, she was firm.

"No, Jason, we really don't need an escort. I know you're perfectly willing, but it just isn't necessary. I heard your father say you all had to be up at four in the morning to go out and check your far range. You can't ride home with us, get back here, and be in any shape to get up at four in the morning!" Only by laughing did Autumn manage to keep Jason from mutinying right then and there. He had counted on riding home with April. But now she added her agreement to Autumn's.

"She's right, Jason. Besides, you know we're going to the town square dance tomorrow night. You'd better be fresh if you think you can outdance me!" It was her appeal rather than Autumn's that convinced him.

But long after they were gone, he wondered. Didn't Autumn like him, or think he was good enough for April? That didn't seem quite right. She had always been friendly to him. He scratched his head. Women, he'd never understand them! Oh, well, tomorrow was the square dance — he'd see April again then.

The two girls rode silently down the lane toward the cutoff to the Wellses' ranch. April stole glances at Autumn, wondering if she should speak. At last the silence was too much for her.

"Autumn, are you angry with me?" It was the sound of a child, a little girl asking her big sister the question, not an equal-to-equal inquiry.

"Angry? Should I be?"

Suddenly April felt miserable without even knowing why. "You're so strange. If I've done something wrong, can't you tell me what's the matter?"

Autumn drew a deep breath. All right, April had asked for it. She kept her voice even, her eyes straight ahead between her horse's ears. "Do you think you're being quite fair to Jason?"

"To Jason!" April's voice came in a weak gasp. Her mind was whirling. "You mean, because I don't know who I am? He knows." She caught the quick look Autumn shot at her. "Oh, he won't tell me. He agrees with you and Dr. McBain that I need to re-member on my own."

In spite of herself Autumn felt a thrill of warm appreciation for the young man. Evidently he cared a lot for April, perhaps was even in love with her. What better way to get her gratitude, perhaps even her love, by being the one to tell who she really was? He must have thought it all out and rejected any such notion. Autumn was glad he hadn't proved to be weak in this.

"Of course not because of who you are. But what about Dr. McBain?"

"Dr. McBain!" April felt like a parrot repeating the words, but what on earth was Autumn talking about? What did Dr. McBain have to do with her feelings for Jason? She wasn't to find out. Before she could gather her wits and ask, they had reached the turnoff from the ranch. Someone was waiting for them there, a dark-browed man with a beard and his hat pulled low. April caught his words.

"My woman, she's sick. I rode into town and they said you were out here. Would you take just a little time and come see her?"

Strange, the pulse that beat in Autumn's throat. He was only a stranger with a sick wife, he needed help. The two girls turned their horses and followed him down the side road that led to a trail into the canyons.

Somewhere the telephone was ringing. Jason Wells fought off sleep to get to it. It was Maxine at the hospital.

"Jason, I hate to bother you, but did the girls decide to spend the night there?"

Jason brushed sleep from his eyes, trying to clear his thoughts. "Why, no. They left here just when they said they would. Have you called them at home? What time is it, anyway?" He craned his neck to see the clock in the corner. "Three o'clock! They should have been there hours ago."

Maxine caught her breath. "They? Didn't you come back with them?"

Jason was wide awake now. Something cold was filling him inside, hoarsening his voice. "They wouldn't let me." He went on to tell Maxine what had happened.

Her voice was serious. "Jason, get in your truck and drive in. You may find them along the way. I'm really worried. Those girls have never broken their word, ever. When they say nine o'clock, they mean nine, and not even one minute after. They aren't home — Letty's there waiting. I can't leave the hospital, neither can Dr. Archer. Our maternity patient can't wait. See what you can find out and then come to the hospital."

Click. The connection was broken, leaving Jason staring at the phone.

In silence he got into his clothes and heavy boots. Even while he had been talking with Maxine, a summer storm had come up, a real gully-washer. Great! The road would be mud, solid mud. The lightning flashes followed by roars of thunder accompanied him as he went down, deciding to use the jeep instead of the truck.

At the last minute he had scrawled a note, leaving it on the dining-room table. When the folks got up they'd find it. He checked his watch. Three-ten. Funny. If it hadn't been for the call, he'd have been getting up in less than an hour anyway. Well, they wouldn't be out on the range today, not in this stuff.

The huge, spattering raindrops had cooled off the night. Jason couldn't be sorry about the storm. They needed the rain. But of all times for it to come! It would wash out every track on the road. The thought set him tingling. Had he already unconsciously begun to think of having to look for tracks? Then it meant he felt as did Maxine that something had happened to the girls.

He laughed at himself, started the jeep, and headed for town. Nothing could happen. Not in or around Dale, it never had! For one thing, there were no strangers. Another thing — where could anyone go if they did commit a crime? The one major highway out of town could be blocked off immediately and the only alternative was ranch roads and canyon trails. It would take an expert in the canyon country to ever pull off anything in Dale! Later he would think of that and wonder. But for now, all he could do was drive toward town — hoping to see two girls with horses who, for some unaccountable reason, had been delayed.

Was that the alarm clock so soon? Dr. McBain felt he had just got into bed. It had been a good drive from Dale to Salt Lake City. He had never before noticed how beautiful it really was. After a late dinner he'd looked up his old college chum and they had talked shop for hours. Their conversation ranged from the new types of sutures to the latest advances in surgery.

But finally his colleague confessed, "I've got to get some sleep if I'm going to give any kind of lecture at all in the morning."

Yet long after Dr. McBain had gone to his room, their conversation remained in his mind. His friend had accused him of burying his talents in Dale.

Matt McBain had only laughed. "Just because people choose to live in small towns shouldn't mean they should be deprived of good medical care."

Now he smiled, thinking of *his* town, *his* hospital, *his* feeling of being at home in Dale. He remembered how Dr. Archer had warned him Dale might weave its magic spell around him, drawing him to it in invisible ties, until he would never want to go elsewhere. It had already started. He would keep up with the latest advances, attend the conferences, get in specialized practice when he could, but for the most part he belonged to Dale.

Now he reached to shut off the alarm clock. Funny, it hadn't been turned on. He glanced at his watch. Six o'clock. The ringing went on. It took a full minute to realize it was the telephone, not an alarm clock. But at Letty Williams's first words Dr. McBain was wide awake, reaching for his clothes as she talked. There would be no conference for him today. He scrawled a note to his friend, who would read it just before his lecture and smile:

Sorry to miss your lecture. Have been called back to Dale.

Matt

By then Dr. McBain would be a long way toward home. It was pouring rain, a gloomy day. The windshield wipers kept time with his thoughts. He tried to sort out what Letty had told him. He lived the long hours while Letty and Maxine waited, the telephone call to Jason Wells. He rode in memory with Jason in the jeep, slowly looking for any trace of the girls, from the ranch to town — finding nothing. He pictured Dr. Archer and Maxine working to help a new life into the world while their thoughts were torn two ways, between the patient and the two nurses who should have been there helping.

He saw Letty Williams with her light in the window, helping a rain-soaked Jason get out of his wet coat, bringing him something hot to drink, and at last turning to the phone.

"We have to call Dr. McBain." He could see Letty blaming herself when there was no way she could have done anything different. He could see Jason Wells's white face showing how much he was in love with April.

But the one thing Dr. McBain could not and would not allow himself to do was speculate on what had happened to the girls. He had miles to drive before reaching Dale. He forced his attention to the road, the same road which had seemed beautiful the day before, but now was only an impediment to his being where he wanted to be.

At last the endless journey was over. He pulled the mud-spattered car into the driveway at the Dale place, to be met at the door by Jason and Letty.

"Is there any word?" Matt asked.

It was Jason who answered. Jason, who

had left behind any sign of childishness in the night hours of worry. Jason, who had been out all morning, looking, searching, to no avail. Jason, who had timed the doctor's arrival correctly. His voice was steady, his face set like a granite rock.

"The rain has hidden any trace. I couldn't even find footprints in our own yard, much less on the road. If whoever planned this had hoped for an effective cover he couldn't have done better if he'd been in league with the devil himself. It's as if April and Autumn vanished into thin air!"

Chapter 11

The bearded stranger with the low-pulled hat chuckled to himself as he led the way down the dusty canyon trail. It had been almost too easy. Furtively he cast a weather eye at the sky. Yep, they were in for a storm! Couldn't be better if he had made it to order. By the time anyone missed the girls, all tracks would be gone, washed away in the thick red mud which appeared when it rained in this country.

Quint Reed thought of how many times he had slipped into town. His first thought had been to catch April alone, but after a few unseen trips, he realized it would be impossible. She was never alone. Either Autumn or that Wells guy would be with her. Summer was getting on. It was July now. He'd have to make his move soon.

He also knew from his night visits and eavesdropping under opened windows this was the week Dr. McBain was gone. Good!

That meant the ride-out calls would be handled by the girls. He had watched the twins like a hawk, and today was perfect.

"I don't remember a cabin out this way." Autumn's voice was not particularly worried, only questioning.

A look of cunning came into the man's eyes. He didn't want them getting suspicious. Deliberately he made his voice smooth, pleasant.

"My woman and me, we been doin' a little prospectin'. We found an old cabin, fixed it up some." He laughed. "Don't expect nothin' fancy, but it's clean."

April had been following in silence, noting the shadows from the rocks were growing longer. It was getting late. In spite of the midsummer long evenings, when the sun went down in this country, it was dark — immediately. Now she leaned forward with a start, grasping her reins tighter.

That voice, it was so familiar! Where could she have heard it? She studied the back of their leader, puzzling over the rough clothes, the profile of beard and slouch hat, and shook her head. She must be mistaken. She didn't know this man. But as the shadows threw longer and longer patches of shade on the path, she grew uneasy. Should she say anything to Autumn? She couldn't see Autumn was concerned over the long ride. But then, Autumn was used to calls into the canyon country.

April had no way of knowing Autumn was beginning to have second thoughts about this particular call. At first she had been thinking about her earlier conversation with her sister. April had sounded absolutely amazed that Dr. McBain would object to her spending so much time with Jason Wells. April couldn't have forgotten how jealous men could be, could she? Autumn shrugged, but as the air cooled and she pulled her thin sweater over her shoulders, she came sharply back to the present.

"Just how much further is it?"

The man in front seemed not to hear.

Autumn stopped her horse, nearly causing a collision from April behind her. "I said, how much further is it?"

The man swung around. "Not much now, miss."

For a moment Autumn was awed by the strange light in his eyes, the wildly standing hair under his old hat. "Perhaps we'd better wait and come back tomorrow when it's lighter, easier to see the trail."

He shook his head. "Beggin' your pardon, but my old woman's feeling mighty poorly. She needs you."

How wise he was! Counting on her feeling of duty as a nurse to go where needed.

"Well, all right." Her voice was still doubtful. "But I hope we get there soon, it looks like rain."

"Oh, we will. It isn't far at all now."

They had come a long way from the cutoff to the Wells ranch, but the girls had been lost in their own thoughts. Their horses were capable, picking their way along the canyon trails. Autumn looked around. Funny, she didn't seem to remember ever being in this part of the canyons before.

"Just where are we?"

Quint Reed's shoulders stiffened but it was too dark for the girls to see. "We're in that little blind canyon near Cedar Breaks."

Cedar Breaks! They really had come a way. Autumn thought of the times she had been there, remembering the scrubby tree growth, interspersed with red rock. But what was this about a blind canyon? She rode on, but was more and more troubled. An unbidden thought crossed her mind. What if something happened to this man? Could she find the way out for herself and April? She doubted it. Why hadn't she been watching more closely?

The first big raindrop spattered the dust in front of her horse's hooves, raising a little whirlpool. It was followed by another, then another.

"For heaven's sake, when will we get there?" Autumn's voice was angry. Why hadn't this backwoods hick told them how far it was? Neither of them were dressed for a canyon jaunt at night, especially in the rain!

But before he could answer it started, a real downpour. It rained as it can rain only in the southern Utah desert country. Drops with the force of marbles blended together to make a torrent.

"Can't we find some shelter?"

Quint Reed yelled back. His face looked white in the storm. "We'd better go on — not safe under trees in an electric storm."

It was April who caught the difference in his speech. Her eyes widened. There wasn't a trace in his last remark of the earlier dialect. Why was he bluffing, pretending to be some prospector or something? Fear shot through her. Who was this man who seemed so familiar, who was leading them off into the night, into a blind canyon, to a cabin with a sick woman?

Or was there even a sick woman? A streak of lightning lighted up the man's face, the dark coat, the pulled-down hat, but most of all the eyes. April stuffed her hand to her mouth to keep from crying out. He was no prospector, no desert rat. He was the man from the hospital who had trailed her. His name was Quint Reed!

What should she do? She had to tell Autumn, but there was no talking in this storm. Thunder crashed until you would have to scream to be heard. Something inside April warned, *Don't let him know you recognize him.* She closed her eyes, forcing herself to think back, to check out her first impressions. Yes, he was the same size. The beard was new, so was the long hair, but the man leading them was definitely Quint Reed!

Slowly the horses plodded ahead. The trail beneath their feet was a river of red mud, slippery, dangerous. To the left was a sharp dropoff into the deep canyon itself. April shuddered to think what would happen if a horse slipped. It would be instant death. No matter who or what this man was, they had to stay with him. There wasn't even enough room on the trail now to turn around. Just when she was sure she couldn't stand it for one more moment, when she thought she would scream to high heaven, they rounded a sharp bend and cut off to the right.

The trail was wider, more comfortable, not so slippery. Then it opened out into a tiny valley. Through the darkness the girls couldn't see how large the valley was, but it was a relief to get away from that dropoff into sheer space. A flash of lightning illuminated a little cabin back against the red rock wall.

Thank God we made it over that trail! Autumn slumped with relief, turning to see that April was all right. The next moment a strong intuition went through Autumn. Why wasn't there a light on in the cabin? Even a sick woman would have lighted a lantern or candle. But the cabin was dark.

They were at the porch now. Autumn caught in a lightning flash signs of recent work and felt better. Evidently the man had been truthful about fixing up the cabin.

"Go right on in — my old woman must have fallen asleep."

The girls stiffly got down from their horses. Although both were good riders, it had been a terrible trip down those canyon trails.

The man reached for the reins. "I'll just put these horses up." He gestured to a shacky-booking building nearby. At least it was a place for the horses to be dry.

Autumn pushed open the creaky door, wishing for at least a flashlight. The minute she stepped inside, she knew it was empty.

Even before April gasped, "There's no one here!"

Autumn looked around, waiting for the next flash of lightning. When it came, she saw an old lantern on a shelf, matches near it. Crossing to it, stumbling over a rough stool on the floor, she managed to light it.

Its flame was flickering, insufficient to drive back shadows into the corners, but enough to confirm the fact the cabin was empty. Two bunks in the corner held blankets; surprisingly enough, they were neatly folded. It was clean, that was something. But why had they been brought there?

April stepped closer to Autumn, whispering low, "That man. Autumn, he's the man I told you about, the one in Salt Lake City. His name is Quint Reed."

But before Autumn could take it into her reeling mind, the door opened and he stood there, menacing, grinning evilly, no longer trying to play the part of an uneducated prospector with a sick woman.

"Welcome to Reedsville!" With a mighty shove, he shot home the bolt on the door. They were alone in a locked cabin in a lonely valley with a captor they both feared and dreaded more than any other living human being — with Quint Reed.

★ ★ ★

Earlier that day a slightly bent figure of a woman had made her way home to a little cabin perched off the road. She was tired by the time she reached it and yet it was a good tiredness. It had been many months since she had left the little cabin. It was good to be back. A few tears for the past fell as she opened it and cleaned out the accumulation of dust and spiders that had formed in her absence. But for the most part the woman's eyes were clear.

The past was over. What the future might bring was uncertain. But for now it was enough to be back in her own little cabin. By dinnertime it was shining clean. She sat down to her simple meal with satisfaction, glad she had told no one she was coming. Tomorrow was enough time to go back, to meet the townspeople, to make right the things she had done.

She was almost finished when she heard the rhythmic beat of horses' hooves coming along the road past her place. Strange! That road wasn't used anymore. It led down into the canyons, somewhere near Cedar Breaks. Why would anyone be on that road? With quick caution she turned out the lamp on the table. She didn't want anyone to know she was back, not until tomorrow. It was enough tonight to be home.

Peering from her freshly washed window she saw them — three horses. The lead horse was ridden by a stranger. She didn't recognize him. The other two were handled by — why, it was Autumn Dale and the girl they called April! What would they be doing riding single file like that on a late July evening down this old road? Had they heard she was back?

She shrank back, some of her newfound confidence melting. Almost she cried out, then muffled the sound. April glanced indifferently at her cabin, not really noticing it. She had never been there, wouldn't have recognized the place. If Autumn hadn't been so busy with her own thoughts, she would have seen the clean windows — and wondered.

The horses passed, not stopping, not even breaking their trot. The woman in the window leaned against the wall, still trying to make it out. At last her face cleared. Of course! They were nurses. The stranger must be a new neighbor, someone who had come in and settled during the months she had been gone. There must be sickness.

When the lamp was out for the night, the woman lay in bed thinking of all those months, of her own sickness. She had progressed beautifully, they told her. There had been one bad setback when the message came. The man she hadn't seen for a long time wouldn't be back — not ever. He had been killed in a car accident, many miles from there. Yet in spite of the message, or perhaps even because of it, the shadows that once troubled her mind one by one were lifted. She was given work to do and did it well.

And the day came when the doctor smiled, saying, "You can go home now."

They gave her bus fare, not knowing how wildly her heart beat. She had chosen a bus that would get her in during the heat of the day, a time when the streets of Dale were almost deserted. She had been lucky. No one recognized her as she stepped down, asking the bus driver to let her off at the closest point to her home.

Actually, even if some of her acquaintances and neighbors had seen her, they wouldn't have recognized her. The pale appearance was gone. She was a rosy-cheeked woman, not old, just a little tired from the journey. Her eyes were clear. She held herself straighter. That is, she did until she neared her cabin, when the heavy travel case she had been given had weighed her down.

It was so good to be home! Then why

couldn't she settle down and sleep?

At last she realized it. She was waiting for something. For the sound of horses' hooves going back past her place, showing that all was well, the nurses were on their way back to the hospital. But the waiting ceased when the storm began. Snug in her own bed she smiled, knowing her cabin was old but stormproof. It had seen many storms, both outside and in. Now in spite of the rain, thunder, and lightning, she was at peace, perhaps for the first time since that day so long ago when she had defied her parents and run off with a man who proved to be as shiftless as they had predicted. It was over, and she slept.

It wasn't until the next day she wondered if the nurses had gone home. She hadn't heard a thing, but then she wouldn't have, not in that storm! From somewhere her old cat had appeared, gaunt, half-starved, crying out for attention and food.

"Why, Kitty! I forgot all about you! Where have you been?"

Kitty couldn't tell her how hard the winter had been, with only an occasional meal scrounged here and there, or even how spring and summer hadn't been much better. But he could purr and push against her leg as she fed him, slowly at first, then all he could hold.

It was good to have something alive in the cabin, something to talk to.

"The road is so muddy I think I'll wait until tomorrow to go in town. After all, if no one knows I'm back, no one will be concerned."

All that day the woman and the cat stayed together. There were so many things to do! The surface cleaning of the day before gave way to an intensive scrubbing. By nightfall the place really shone. She had even ripped up an old dress and made curtains for the window, replacing the rags hanging there. The wood stove shone with polish. The nickel beamed brightly. The worn floorboards had been washed to within an inch of their life. When she was finished she was tired, but it was good.

"There's no need for us to live in poverty any longer."

Kitty purred, but a shadow crossed the woman's face for a moment. Feeling the need to confide in someone, the woman absently stroked the cat's fur, much improved by the removal of accumulated burrs.

"Funny, he finally made it, then he died." She thought of the message that had come. Just before the car accident, her husband had struck it rich, not in the earth, but in some kind of deal he had made. No one seemed quite sure of what deal, but no one could prove it wasn't legal, either. There had been money left, enough to keep her for a time, until she could gather her courage and find work. Now she confided in her cat, who listened intently.

"I wish things had been different. If this had come sooner . . ." She was lost in a recital of might-have-beens. But the cat wisely closed his eyes. He knew better.

Suddenly the woman looked outside. The unexpected storm had passed entirely. The road was drying up.

"Tomorrow I'll go into Dale and see them all." A smile softened her face. "They'll be surprised, I can tell you that!"

If only she had known of all the excitement in Dale, the eager ears waiting for news, the eyes refusing to meet other eyes when asking the question, "Any sign of the girls?"

The whole town was upset over the disappearance of Autumn and April. There were absolutely no leads as to where they might have gone, no clues.

And as Dr. McBain, Jason, Letty, and the others prepared for another sleepless night, the only person who knew anything of the girls' whereabouts lay asleep in her spotless cabin not far from town. If anyone had thought about her it would have been to remember she had been gone since the fall before. No one would have dreamed the clue to the disappearance lay with a woman who had come back to her own cabin, come back with clear mind and determination — a woman named Mrs. Jimson.

Chapter 12

The woman entered the waiting room of Big Rock Hospital a little timidly, yet with a smile. She could hardly wait to see everyone. As luck would have it, there were few cases in the hospital just then and Dr. McBain was sitting down for a rare moment, talking with Maxine and Letty. At first they didn't recognize the woman who had come in, then . . .

"Why, Mrs. Jimson, how well you look!" Dr. McBain was on his feet, his grin broad and welcoming.

Letty and Maxine weren't far behind. "When did you get back?"

The woman's face glowed. "I came in day before last. It was so stormy yesterday I just cleaned house and stayed home but was glad when it cleared off. The roads in front of my place get awfully muddy!"

"Well, you sure are looking great. Welcome home."

Tears sprang to Mrs. Jimson's face. "I just

had to come and tell you how sorry I was for all the trouble I caused last fall . . ." Her voice broke, but Letty put an arm around her.

"Don't worry about it at all. No one blames you, not even Annie Wells. She only said, 'The good Lord knows if I had lost a baby like Mrs. Jimson did, I might have felt the same way.' In fact, she's kept track of your progress. Every time Dr. McBain dropped over to see you, he had to report to Annie. She hopes you'll come out and see her and Faith when you feel like it."

It was a long speech for Letty. Usually her sentences were short, crisp, to the point. But she felt Mrs. Jimson needed assurance. She was rewarded.

The woman's face lit up. "I really will. It's good to be back." She looked around and her face fell with disappointment. "I'd hoped the girls would be here but I suppose they were all tired out from their ride-out call the other night."

Dr. McBain's face had gone rigid. "Girls? You mean Autumn and April?"

"Why, yes! I saw them go past night before last, just before the big storm broke."

The next moment Matthew McBain's hands were gripping her arms in a viselike grip. "You *saw* them? Were they alone? They went past *your* place?"

A tongue of fear licked at Mrs. Jimson. "Yes, they went past. But they weren't alone. They were following a man."

Dr. McBain looked into her eyes. "Mrs. Jimson, Autumn and April have been missing since leaving the Wells ranch after supper night before last."

"Missing! But they aren't missing — they went past my place, I tell you!" She stared at them all, looking frightened. "I didn't go to sleep for a long time. I thought they'd probably be riding back. Then the storm came and I figured they would stay over with the man and his family." Again she broke off.

Dr. McBain had released her and was leading her across the room to a chair. "Now Mrs. Jimson, tell us exactly what happened and the time as near as you can make it out."

Mrs. Jimson furtively rubbed her arms where his tight grip had left red marks, unwilling to let him know he had hurt her. "I had just finished eating, but it was later than usual. Must have been between six-thirty and seven. I heard horses and ran to the window, wondering if someone were coming to my cabin." A flush went through her face. "I didn't go out, it was my first night home. I just felt I needed one night to get used to things here again."

Letty nodded at her encouragingly and

Maxine smiled. Mrs. Jimson wrinkled her brow trying to remember.

"The man wore an old hat pulled down. I think he had a beard. They rode on down the old road, it leads somewhere into the canyons, near Cedar Breaks. I wondered why they were going, then decided someone must have come in and settled up past me during the time I was gone."

She stopped, then asked, "Don't you think . . . don't you think it was a ride-out call?"

Matt shook his head. "No, Mrs. Jimson. We don't. To our knowledge no one has moved in past you. We don't know anything except the girls left the Wells ranch the other night right after dinner. That would make it just about right for passing your place when they did. The stranger must have met them near the cutoff to the Wells ranch. Maybe he really is living down in those canyons, but I doubt it."

The next moment he was at the phone calling the Wells ranch. "Jason?" He repeated Mrs. Jimson's story. "Get in here as fast as you can, will you?"

But Maxine Phillips had remained silent long enough. "Dr. McBain, my Sancho knows every inch of the canyons around here. He will be back from Kanab in a few hours. Wait for him. If anyone on earth can find the girls in those canyons, it will be Sancho!" Her dark eyes glowed. "He will be proud to help you. Ever since you stitched his arm he's felt in debt to you."

"It may mean taking time off from work, Maxine."

Her steady gaze never wavered. "In this town any man would be happy to either take or give time off from work to look for the girls. This is Dale, remember, Dr. McBain?"

For perhaps the first time Matthew understood the close ties of the little community, the old-fashioned working together in time of need. He could feel a stinging sensation back of his eyes, hot, prickly.

"Thank you, Maxine. As soon as Sancho gets back, we'll start." He smiled at Mrs. Jimson. "Thanks to you we know where to begin! With the storm erasing any trace of tracks, we had no idea which direction to even begin looking, although Jason and I spent most of yesterday out looking."

He crossed to Mrs. Jimson. "You'll never know what you've done for me . . . for us."

She smiled quietly. It was his way of telling her how very important she was in Dale. She had needed it. In spite of all her assurance, until she had come to the hospital and seen for herself there was no memory of her wild actions those months before, it would have been impossible to rest.

Dr. McBain looked at her speculatively. "In fact, Annie Wells just may owe you a debt of gratitude."

"Annie Wells?"

"Yes, I strongly suspect her oldest son Jason is madly in love with April." He didn't see the startled exchange of glances between Maxine and Letty. They were both aware of Autumn's plans for April, without her ever having said anything. So Jason Wells was in love with April! Now, wasn't that interesting! The same thought crossed their minds. That left Dr. McBain for Autumn, perhaps. Good! April was young for her years, a better companion for Jason than for Dr. McBain, who needed a full-grown woman, not a girl.

There was no more time for speculation just then. The door crashed open, and a man staggered in. He had been thrown from his horse when it was spooked. A crude bandage only partially stopped the steady flow of blood from his head wound. In minutes he was in the other room, Maxine and Letty both helping Dr. McBain take care of it.

First the doctor had to explain, "Head

wounds always look worse than they are. There are hundreds of tiny blood vessels just under the scalp which bleed freely when you get cut. Nothing to be alarmed about." His deft fingers cleaned, anesthetized, and stitched the cut. It took twelve stitches.

When he was through, he washed the man's face, then handed him a mirror. "Pretty good seamstress, huh?"

The man even laughed, then swayed. He had lost some blood before getting there.

"Put him to bed for overnight. There shouldn't be any problem but he needs the rest." He grinned and left the room, hearing Letty override the rider's protest he was okay, and he'd undress himself thank you!

Letty was more than able to handle it herself. He wasn't needed. In a flash his mind returned to the girls. Jason Wells was just getting out of the jeep. Good, they could leave when Sancho returned.

"Can you handle everything?" Dr. McBain made the mistake of asking Dr. Archer, Maxine, and Letty just before leaving a few hours later. They were all standing in the waiting room. Jason and Sancho were waiting outside. They had traded the jeep for horses. No jeep could get into the canyons on the route they would have to take. Matt wasn't prepared for Dr. Archer's roar.

"We handled it for a good many years before you came, didn't we?" But the old man's ferocity was overshadowed by the twinkle in his eyes, quickly replaced by concern. "Don't come back until you find them. Those girls are precious to this whole town."

Again Dr. McBain felt that same stinging sensation he had earlier. How the Dale twins were loved! His face went hot at his unconscious and silent postscript, *especially by me.* There was no time to stand around mooning. They had a job to do, a big job. But the memory of the faithful three waving to them from the porch of Big Rock Hospital stayed in Dr. McBain's mind long after he turned his horse away from town and obediently followed Sancho Phillips and Jason Wells down the dusty road leading to Mrs. Jimson's cabin — and the canyons beyond.

While the town of Dale was up in arms over the girls' disappearance, the girls were going through experiences they wouldn't have dreamed possible.

At one point April told Autumn, "If I saw all this happening in a movie, I'd laugh and call it pure melodrama. But it's really happening, and to us!"

When Quint Reed had barred the door and turned toward them that first night in the storm, it was with huge enjoyment of the coup he had just pulled off.

"Welcome to Reedsville!" He tore off the soaking wet hat and coat he'd left on to attend to the horses and threw them on a chair. "Looks like you guests could at least have started the fire." He touched a match to the kindling. The well-laid fire caught, throwing grotesque patterns into the shadows that had not been reached by the paler lantern light.

"Just why have you brought us here?" Autumn had found her voice. She was afraid, terribly afraid of this man, but there was April to think of.

Quint's face leered at them. "Why, I thought it was time for us to have a cozy little talk, you and me and my fiancee there." He pointed to April.

Autumn's tongue was paralyzed by sheer fury. What a rotten thing to have happen! April had been doing so well, remembering at her own speed. Would this throw her back into forgetfulness in order to block out the pain? She was staring at Quint, her hand at her throat.

"Fiancee? You must be out of your mind! I've never seen you before except in Salt

Lake City in the hospital and then when you followed me!" April's words rang with truth. Even Quint Reed was forced to admit there was no recognition whatsoever in her eyes. But neither would he admit defeat.

"We'll see about that. You were engaged to me long before Salt Lake City, Miss Uppity! When you've been here as my guest for a few weeks, I think you'll remember. You'll be glad enough to marry me then."

If April caught the significance of his words, she ignored them. Her look was steady, almost unafraid. Autumn marveled. Was this the weak girl who had come to them, the dependent one? She was standing up to Quint with every ounce of strength she had.

"That would be quite impossible. In the first place we won't be here even a few days. You think you can keep us here? Just try it!"

Autumn tried to find her voice to warn April not to inflame him. But it was no use. April's words outscreamed the storm although she spoke in a normal voice.

"The second reason is that I will never marry any man on earth except Jason Wells!"

If Quint Reed was astounded at the words, it was no more than Autumn. Jason Wells? Like a flashback of memory came April's words:

191

"He's tall and strong. When I'm with him I feel as if nothing in the world could hurt me. He wants to spend the rest of his life in Dale. That's fine with me. We can do a great deal of good here."

With a mighty crash everything fell into place. Of course! Jason Wells had signed a teaching contract. Autumn visualized April's face earlier that evening, her genuine puzzlement over Autumn's concern that her association with Jason could hurt Dr. McBain.

Then, then there was no reason why Autumn herself should hold back her love. Or was there? She closed her eyes and swallowed hard, forgetting their peril for a moment, remembering the seeming disinterest about April when the doctor's name had come up; the continued glow in Dr. McBain's eyes when he thought Autumn wasn't noticing. Everything was crystal clear. Dr. McBain had been truthful. He loved her. Not April, but her! It was too wonderful to be true.

A roar of rage returned her to the cabin in the storm. Quint was staring at April, his face twisted, all his fine dreams shattered. His voice was thick as he started toward her.

"I'll show you who you'll marry!" His breath came in quick gasps, through clenched teeth. "After I'm through with you, Jason Wells or no one else will want you! I'll keep you here and force you to scrub floors." His laugh made Autumn's skin crawl. "And other household duties."

For the moment he had forgotten Autumn, forgotten everything except April's scornful dismissal of all the castles he had built that lonely winter.

April stood her ground, proud but pale. The thought of Jason's love, the feeling of proclaiming it aloud for the first time, had given her unbelievable strength.

But Autumn's strength was not from love. It came from the adrenalin flowing through her, triggered by fear. She could see insanity in Quint Reed's face. He was on the brink. She sprang between April and the maddened man.

"Leave her alone! I tell you, leave her alone!"

He stopped for a moment. The madness disappeared, but in its place cold hatred shone from his eyes. "You! It was your fault all along! Swinging around so smart, asking a man to make a pass, then protesting! If you had stayed out of it, none of this would have happened!" He seized her shoulders until the fingers bit into her flesh.

She jerked free, screaming at him, "You beast! You rotten animal!"

She heard a gasp behind her. She couldn't

see April's face, but Quint Reed could. It was enough to stop him in his tracks. There was returning memory, accusation. Autumn's words, a faithful replay of a scene in the past, had torn aside the final curtain of her memory.

"I remember! I remember it all!" She advanced on him.

Unbelievingly he fell back from her. She was splendid, magnificent, all the adjectives one could ever think of, as she accused him.

"Yes, I was engaged to you. But you couldn't even leave my own twin sister alone!" She didn't hear Autumn's quick cry. She was too intent on Quint Reed.

"Get out! Get out and never come back! I told you once that I never wanted to see you again. Now I hate you more than any other person on earth!"

Never had Autumn heard such scorn. It seemed to shrivel Quint, to freeze him to the spot, to rob him of speech. Quietly she slipped behind him, unlocked the door, and opened it wide. When the time came, she would be ready.

April could not hold him at bay forever with her words. When he recovered, he would be worse than ever, knowing every plan was useless.

But April wasn't through. "Do you know what you did to me? Do you know that I left my parents? They came to look for me and were killed on the way."

It was a cry of despair, almost more than Autumn could bear. She made an involuntary motion to stop April. Then her nurse's training came to her. Let April get it out of her system for once and for all. It would be more healing in the long run.

"I spent weeks and months wondering who I was, not knowing anyone. I didn't care if I lived or died. Why should I? If you haven't anything to live for, what's the use?"

April didn't see how hard she had hit him with her words. In that moment Quint Reed saw himself for what he really was. Realization was terrible. His plan had failed. Even if he could force the girl to her knees he would still have lost. She would hate and despise him forever. It was a blow to his self-esteem. At that moment the so-called love he had built around his little plan evaporated. In its place the same hatred he felt for Autumn began to grow.

Autumn saw it, the exact moment when he began to recover. It was now or never. In an instant she was beside her twin, only this time with a mighty shove she rammed full force into Quint Reed. Only his being off-guard saved her. He had been expecting nothing of the sort.

Before he could regain his balance he was flying through the open door, out into the stormy night. This time when the heavy bolt shot home inside the door, the girls were alone, safe at least for the time being, while their kidnapper sprawled flat in a puddle of muddy red water at the foot of the steps outside!

Chapter 13

Autumn turned from the door to meet an onrush. April was in her arms, crying her heart out. Now that the immediate danger was held off, reaction had set in. Autumn just let her cry. It was the best therapy she could give her sister.

"You were my real sister, my twin, all along!" April's sobs had given way to hiccups and incoherent speech. "How could you keep from telling me?"

"I had to." The three words gave April the full extent of Autumn's pain all those long months. "Dr. McBain said you must remember on your own. You must not try to force it, but let it come naturally." Tears filled Autumn's own eyes. "Then for this to happen!"

April sat up and pushed the brown hair back from her face. "I'm glad it did."

Autumn was speechless.

April looked into her sister's eyes. "It's

worth whatever happens to know who I am and — and that I do belong!" This time the tears were of joy.

It was a long time before the girls noticed the ominous silence outside the cabin. The happiness of April had completely over-ridden any thought of the man so rudely ejected from his own cabin, the man who even now would be planning some new horror against them.

Autumn had seen in her quick glance around the cabin the sturdy shutters locked from the inside. Quint Reed had done his work well. The cabin was safe from attack. He had made it almost into a jail. But what a well-stocked jail! Cupboards full of food. Dishes. Pans to cook with in the fireplace.

Suddenly April giggled. "As long as we had to be kidnapped, we were certainly kid-napped deluxe!"

Autumn joined in.

It was the last straw for the man outside in the rain, the peals of laughter that somehow escaped even through the heavy walls and door of the cabin. Quint knew he would not be able to get in. A little grin of satisfaction crossed his face. Fine! There was something else he could do.

Quietly he slipped to the shelter and found a place that was relatively dry. He would bide his time until morning and then . . . his smile was unpleasant. But it was a satisfied man who slept in the scanty shelter that night, thinking of just what he would do the next day.

Quint's plans were hampered the next morning by the weather. While the thunder and lightning had stopped, the rain continued during the morning. It was late afternoon before he could carry out his promise to himself. He was hugely enjoying himself now. His twisted brain had found a way for revenge. He wouldn't kill the girls, not that. He didn't want to be a murderer. But he would give them a good scare. April heard it first, the whinnying of horses. She rushed to a shutter, opening it just enough to catch a glimpse of the outside.

"Good-bye girls!" Quint Reed was mounted on his horse, his evil face contorted in a huge smile as he waved at the partly opened shutter. But his procession did not end there. *Behind his own horse were tied the horses the girls had ridden into the canyon.*

Autumn ran to the door. "What are you doing with our horses?"

A mocking laugh was his only answer. With a flourish Quint dug his heels into the horse's sides. The last they saw of him was when he rounded the bend that led out of the little valley to the tortuous trail out of the canyon.

"How can any man be so rotten?" April was white to the lips. "Can we get out?"

Autumn's answer was slow, deliberate. "We can probably get out, but it's going to take time, April. There were dozens of trails cutting off from that one. It was so dark I couldn't even see which ones we were taking. That's what he's counting on. By the time we can get out of here, he'll be far away and safe." Her even tones didn't fool April one bit.

"And if we don't get out, he will shave off his beard, cut his hair, and no one will ever be the wiser." She shuddered. "To think, I could have married him!"

"No, you never could have married him. I think even if he hadn't shown his hand, you would have realized in time what he was." Autumn laughed, the first joyful sound since they had left the Wells ranch. "I will have to admit, Jason Wells is quite an improvement!"

April blushed, showing her happiness. "Now you can quit preaching to me about Dr. McBain!"

Autumn managed to keep her voice cool. "What do you mean?"

"Well, now that I've remembered everything, he won't care one bit that Jason and I are engaged. He'll think it's great."

Autumn turned away to hide her relief. So all April thought of her concern for Matt McBain was he had been worried over her memory loss. Good! She need not ever know of Autumn's plans for her.

"I wonder if we should start out tonight or wait?" April said. "You know, Quint might just be waiting around a bend or something."

It was something Autumn hadn't considered. "Let's wait until morning. This red mud is so slippery it's going to be hard walking anyway."

Now that Quint was gone, there was no need to keep the shutters closed. The only entrance into the valley was the way they had come. There was a sparsity of vegetation — stunted cedars, a little sagebrush. Nothing to hide a man with or without a horse. If he attempted to come back, they would see him. In moments the shutters were open and sunlight streaming in. A little breeze had come up and it was even pleasant.

"You know." April sounded dreamy. "I wouldn't mind spending a honeymoon here."

Autumn stared at her twin. "A honeymoon! Here?" She looked around the little room.

"Sure. Think of the privacy."

Autumn laughed out loud. "You get your memory back one night and the next day already you're the irrepressible April Dale everyone knew!"

"April Dale. You don't know how good it is to have a last name. Autumn." She paused. "I don't ever want to talk about it again, but — do you blame me for our parents' death?"

"No, April. They wanted to come. I'm only sorry you didn't get to see them again."

The twins were quiet a long time. When April spoke, it was as if she had closed that chapter of her life forever. "Well, April Dale may sound nice, but April Wells is nicer, and if I have my way, before September that's what it's going to be."

"So soon?"

"Why not? As soon as Jason knows I know who I am, he'll ask me to marry him. We can have a honeymoon before his teaching contract starts. It's only practical to look ahead, isn't it?"

Autumn threw up her hands.

"If Jason knew what a handful he was going to have, maybe he'd run instead of

202

proposing!" She sobered. "Seriously, April. Jason is a wonderful man. You'll have a good life."

April didn't look at Autumn as she asked, "What about you? Why don't you find someone, Dr. McBain, maybe?" Her voice was just a shade too casual.

"Oh, heavens. Do you think the great Matthew McBain would ever look at me?"

"Yes, I do. I've seen him look at you."

Autumn's face took on the hated telltale red.

"Aha! So that's it, Autumn. What did you do, put him off on my account?" April didn't know how close she had come to Autumn's secret. "Well, you needn't, not one minute longer. I'm all well and intend to grab Jason before anyone else does." Was she really that naive or just tactful? Autumn didn't know.

"Come on," Autumn said. "Let's find something to eat and get packed." It was a hard job. They could only take what they could carry. Luckily, they did find two old gunnysacks.

"We'll have to take enough food to carry us through but it can't be heavy."

They settled on all the bar chocolate, instant tea, and instant orange juice they could find. They baked biscuits in the dutch oven in the fireplace. They were easier to carry than bread. They did find an old water canteen and filled it with clean water. In the morning they would refill it. Luckily the rains had stopped. Their sweaters would prove enough to keep off the night air with the help of a blanket apiece from the bunks. But when they were up and ready, Autumn looked at their gear doubtfully. "It doesn't seem like very good rations."

"It's the best we can do." April was determined. They were starting a long miserable journey. Whether they would make it was doubtful. But they had to make it! She thought of Jason, Dr. McBain, Letty, Maxine, the others. They must be going through torment now wondering where the girls were. "Let's go."

It was two silent girls who shouldered the awkward sacks and started across the clearing to the trail out of their little valley. Once they left it, they were also leaving the security of food and shelter, even water.

Autumn took a long breath, then faced away, looking back no more. There was no alternative. Too well she knew how many canyons there were, how many little draws. Even if their friends knew which direction they had come, how could they ever be found in that secluded valley? She thought of Dr. McBain, Jason, the others, knowing their anxiety. *We have to make it. We have to. At least we're together.*

Autumn's last thought was short-lived. They had walked for several hours, gaining the ledge leading upwards, out of the canyon, when they rounded a bend. Face down in the trail lay a man — Quint Reed. For a moment they stopped still, wondering if it were a trick. But the trickle of blood on his hand, the grotesque angle of his body were not tricks. He was hurt. Instantly all thought of anything except being needed left them. Quint was injured, badly.

Autumn's glance took in the scene. "Look!" The rain must have weakened the ledge. Something had started it sliding. A great hole was torn from the trail, probably twenty feet across. Boulders were scattered along it on each side, with a path showing the descent of a great deal of red earth into the seemingly bottomless canyon below.

Autumn shuddered. "He must have been caught in it, or else tried to lead the horses around it." She peered over the edge. A jagged piece of cloth clung to a sturdy cedar clump still firmly rooted. "He was saved by those. They broke his fall and he must have dragged himself up to the trail." Quint's eyes flickered. Autumn had seen the same expression once in the eyes of a dog that had been hit by a car. Anguish, pleading.

He managed to raise his head. "Help me." The next moment merciful oblivion gave him rest from his terrible injuries.

Autumn and April looked at one another. As had happened so often in the past, their thoughts meshed perfectly.

"We can't leave him here, he will die," Autumn said. Anyone else would have just taken for granted he would die whether or not they left him. Not these two, bred in the canyon country, raised with compassion.

"He's a human being first, then a patient, no matter who he is," April said. "One of us will have to stay."

"Only one of us?" Autumn said.

"Yes, only one of us. If we both stay, we'll all die, especially with that slide."

Autumn followed April's pointing finger. There was nothing to show the slide had occurred *after* three travelers had crossed it and not ages before. Even if a rescue party came this way, they wouldn't dream anyone would be on the other side. The horses were gone, either swept away by the slide, or spooked and run off into one of the many branching canyons. There was no hope in that direction.

Autumn's lips were white. "We'll get him back to the cabin. Without our horses we don't even have a medical kit."

But April shook her head. "It will take hours to do that. We need all the time we can get. Help me drag him over to that clump of stunted cedars and out of the sun. I can go back to the cabin later and get more food and water. We can't take the time to get him back."

Her voice almost broke, but she fiercely held up her chin. "We've got to get you across there and out of here!" Never once did she betray the feeling she had of being left alone with a dying man, a dying enemy, or the fear of seeing her newly discovered twin sister risking her life to cross that dangerous twenty-foot gap.

Neither did Autumn argue. April knew this country even less than she herself. The memory lapse might have affected place memories, too. They couldn't chance it. Yet to leave her here alone with Quint?

"It has to be done, Autumn." April's hands were unsteady as she took the blankets from the gunnysacks, tying them together. Thank God they were strongly woven Indian blankets. It would be the only thing in their favor, that and the huge boulders still remaining on the hillside of the trail. Would they hold? If they didn't Autumn would be plunged to her death in the canyon below.

There wasn't a trace of fear showing as the girls looped the blanket and threw it to the first boulder. It fell far short. They tried again. This time it caught. From the safety of the firm trail they tugged, to see if it would hold their weight. It did.

Autumn's eyes met April's. "I'll be back as soon as I can. Get to the cabin and find what you need. Do what you can for him. Bring whiskey if you can find it. It may help the pain some." She stopped. "I'm coming back, April. I'm coming back."

She clenched her teeth, held the blanket, and cautiously crept to the big rock. This time there was only one of them to throw, loop, and test the blanket. It caught and held, but as Autumn left its safety for the last step this time using the blanket around a small cedar clump, the second rock lost its hold and plunged into the canyon, taking with it everything in its path, bouncing angrily to the canyon floor far below as if cheated of its victim and madly clanging its disappointment against the rock walls.

Autumn's face was white as she stood on safe ground and called back to April, "Don't forget — I'll be back as soon as I can!"

For one minute April bit her tongue to keep from crying out. "I can't do it — I'm a coward. Come back, Autumn, come back!" She didn't realize until she tasted the sickish taste of blood in her mouth how hard she had set her teeth to keep from uttering those words. One more wave and Autumn was out of sight around the great red-rock wall. April was alone with her charge.

If I think of what she might face, more slides, danger, I'll go mad. I can't do it. I'll get busy, instead. April took her sweater and put it over the injured man's body. Luckily it was a coat sweater, long and warm. It would offer some protection. By the time she could reach the cabin in the valley, get food to replace that which she had sent with Autumn, plus whiskey and water, it would be evening and cool. With a resolute air she set back over the long miles they had come that morning. Yet as she walked, the trail beneath her feet became easier.

April's thoughts were of Jason and the life they would share. She reached the cabin and got what she needed. She also grabbed the matches. There was very little wood she could get, but maybe the sagebrush would burn. It was at least worth a try.

While April struggled back to Quint Reed with her burden, Autumn was forcing her tired feet upward, always upward on the trail. At first she had not found it too hard to keep on the main trail. Now other trails were leading off. It was hard to distinguish one from another. Her climbing had been gradual for a while. Now it was a marathon. She must keep on going. April was depending on her. Step after tired step she took one following another, until she could move no more.

She dropped to a big rock by the trail, ate small pieces of biscuit and chocolate, and sipped the water. Only a few swallows. One canteen of water had to last — who knew how long? Rising wearily she started walking again, walking until it was sheer torture to take even one more step. Only then did she stop, find a small tree for shelter, and drop to the ground, rolled up in a blanket. If only she could sleep forever!

A night owl looked at her curiously, then flew away. She never knew it. Autumn Dale lay exhausted and asleep under a stunted tree on the edge of a red-rock trail. But miles back her twin sister April kept vigil for a dying man whose only recognition had been that one plea, "Help me."

It had been enough to call out the best in her. No longer was he an enemy. In his hours of pain and suffering, she could only feel compassion, wishing she could do more. There was no room for hatred between a dying patient and his nurse.

Chapter 14

It was a grim-faced trio of men who made camp in a small canyon long after the sun had set. They were tired, dusty, and discouraged — at least two of them were. Jason had been elected camp cook. He didn't mind. It gave him something to do as he thought of the fruitless search these last three days. Dr. McBain was tending the fire, carefully hoarding the bits and pieces of scrub cedar they had gathered.

Only Sancho, busy with the horses, seemed in normal spirits. "Tomorrow we'll go on." His dark eyes flashed. "You know, sooner or later we will comb every side canyon. This particular trail dead ends, so we will find the girls if they are here."

If. The word hung in the still night air. What if the girls had come back past Mrs. Jimson's without her seeing them? Then what? Yet it didn't seem likely, in all that storm. No, the best thing to do was go on doing just what they had been doing — side-track from the main trail into every canyon, check it out, then go back and into another.

Dr. McBain sighed. "Well, we'd better eat and get some sleep."

They had first discussed going back to town nights and coming out again in the mornings.

Sancho had vetoed that. "We'll waste too much time 'commuting.' It's better to stay right where we finish searching for the day."

Jason and Matt McBain agreed. Sancho was the expert. They would follow his advice.

Yet at least two of the little search party found sleeping out under the stars didn't help their peace of mind. Once when Jason had mentioned something about April, wondering if she were strong enough to stand the trip into such an area, Dr. McBain smiled.

"You love her, don't you?"

Something in the young man's eyes confirmed his words. "More than life itself."

Without thinking, Matt said, "I feel the same about Autumn."

Wordlessly Jason held out his hand, sympathy meeting sympathy, brothers in their troubled search.

Was it that moment which seemed to give

them new courage? Perhaps. Whatever it was, the next morning when they arose, Sancho stood still for a moment, then said what he had been thinking.

"You know, nearly at the end of this trail, where it just dwindles out against a rock wall, there's a little valley, off to the right. An old prospector built some kind of cabin. I'm wondering if we should give up this canyon trotting and go directly there. It doesn't seem reasonable the man who brought the girls here, if he did, would do so without knowing where he was going. At first I thought maybe his idea was just to get into a canyon. But maybe he's someone who knows this area. If he does, he may have taken them to that old cabin, especially since it was such a stormy night."

Jason and Matt looked at one another.

"Whatever you say, Sancho." Jason's quiet assent reflected Matt's faith in their guide.

They packed their gear and rode back to the main trail. As they went deeper into the canyon, Matt couldn't help but exclaim, "What a trail! And to come over it at night! Can you imagine it?"

Jason's jaw set in a grim line. "What I can imagine is what I'm going to do to whoever this man is who brought them here."

Matt scowled thoughtfully. "You don't

think maybe the man really does have other family down here, someone who was sick?" he asked.

"No, Doc," Sancho said. "If any man had settled here, or were even doing prospecting, and had any family, we would know. In this country you don't go off by yourself. Too much chance of something happening. You want your neighbors to know where you are, in case that something *does* happen." His dark eyes glistened. "I'm not sure what we'll find. I do know that someone is going to be in mighty big trouble. The whole town of Dale is up there waiting for what we find. It will be interesting to see just what they do. One thing, they won't sit back and let some creep go scot-free if he's brought the twins down here for some reason of his own."

Matt McBain shivered at the coldness in Sancho's voice. He hadn't seen this grim side of the happy-go-lucky man before. And Matt, who hated the unknown man, almost felt sorry for him, too. Imagine meeting Sancho and Jason and being led back to face the town of Dale. It wouldn't be pleasant, that was certain.

There were rocks in the path now.

"From the storm," Jason explained. Pebbles, small boulders, even some huge rocks.

The horses carefully skirted them, feeling their way, disliking the sliding gravel beneath their feet. At some places Sancho and Jason motioned for Matt to dismount and lead his horse across. Those rocks could be treacherous.

At last Sancho motioned them to slow and stop. "Just around this next bend is where the trail cuts off into the little valley. We want to take it easy, it's very narrow."

He motioned to the ledge. It looked crumbly, as if the whole trail could slide any minute into the depths of the canyon below.

Matt could see the shine of a small stream at the bottom, dwarfed by distance. To think the girls might have had to ride this — in pitchblack and storm. It was more than he could stand to think of.

Slowly, almost at a standstill, they rounded the bend and there . . .

"My God!" It was not a curse, but a prayer. For over twenty feet the trail had been swept away into the canyon, leaving only the rough hillside with a few huge boulders here and there.

In that instant, as Matt stared into the awful gaping wound in the earth, it seemed his very heart and soul had died. He could see Jason, white-faced, reeling back against his horse. But Sancho would not give up so easily. He knelt to the ground. When he stood, his voice was triumphant.

"Someone has crossed this since the avalanche slide!"

Jason and Matt fell to their knees, staring at the bootprint, with the toe marks pointed *up the trail over which they had just come!*

Sancho's voice was even. "It's a woman's footprint. It was made after the slide. That means they did come here." He paused. "It also means someone is alive on the other side of the slide. It's too far across for her to have made it without some help. If the man had been helping, he would have been the one to come across. It looks to me as if one of the girls made it across and the other is still in there!"

Matt opened his mouth to cry across the chasm, "Autumn!"

But before the word was out, Sancho had gripped his arm. "No! A high shout could start rocks rolling again. We have to go across."

Matt's blood ran cold. One step, and . . . but either Autumn or April had crossed it. So could he.

It wasn't easy. If Sancho hadn't been so expert with his lasso, they wouldn't have made it. But the years of outdoor work, the pride of lassoing, now came to Sancho's aid.

On the first toss he snared his object, a large rock firmly planted well back from the jagged edge of the broken-off trail.

"I'll go first, I'm the lightest." Holding the rope, Sancho inched his way across. "You next, Doc."

It was harder for Matt. He wasn't used to this kind of thing. But he never said a word, just gripped the secured rope and did it. Every time loose gravel moved, the sweat came. By the time he reached the other side, he was soaked. Jason and Sancho admired him more than ever before, and when Jason had come across, they turned into the entrance to the little valley. The first thing they saw was a blanket-covered form, lying still under a scrubby cedar.

Sancho's face filled with compassion. "I'll look."

But Matt McBain moved ahead. "I'm the doctor, it's my duty." For a moment he closed his eyes and clenched his teeth. What — *who* would he find under that blanket? By the unnatural stillness he was sure someone was dead. Even in sleep human bodies do not take on that grotesque quiet.

He turned the blanket back. He had been right. Someone was dead. He had never seen the man before — bearded, long hair. So this was the man who had led the girls here. Who was he? Why had he done this? Was he some kind of pervert?

Dr. McBain's professional eyes took in the position, felt the wrist of the dead man. "He's been dead since probably this morning, no longer than that."

Jason said slowly, "Then someone was here with him until then." He pointed to the kettle still holding water. "We'll go on to the cabin."

Sancho made the decision. "Yes. She would know there was nothing more she could do here."

The longest trip in the world has to end, but to those three looking for sweethearts and friends it seemed this one never would. Yet the moment came when they stood at the edge of the little clearing, seeing the cabin huddled against the opposite wall. This time there was no need to fear starting another slide. All three stared at the cabin. *There was a tiny wisp of smoke curling from the chimney!* They broke into a run. Matt McBain had always prided himself on his speed, had even won college track meets. But this time he was outdistanced. Sancho ran with the grace of a deer, but Jason ran with hope born of desperation.

"April! Autumn!" Their cries filled the clear air, bringing someone to the door — a tired girl who ran to meet them, trouble and weariness forgotten. A brown-haired girl with blue eyes, April Dale.

Straight to Jason she came and into his arms. Sancho and Matt slowed their steps. This meeting was almost holy. They had seen the look on April's face. She had gone through a terrible time. But as Matt and Sancho looked into each other's eyes, there was a burning question.

It was the question April cried out moments later, releasing herself from Jason. "But where is Autumn?"

They could not meet her eyes.

She became almost hysterical. "One of us had to stay. He was hurt so badly. Autumn left. She made it across the slide."

"When?" Dr. McBain's question cracked like a pistol shot.

April had to count back. "This is the fourth day since then." The fourth day! Autumn had left the same day the men had started their search. When they finally got April calmed down, she could tell them more of the story. She told them all that had happened and how she'd stayed with Quint till he died.

Then she asked again. "But where — where is Autumn?"

Sancho was the only one who could meet

her eyes squarely. "We're not sure, April. We started by combing every branch canyon from the main trail. Then we came straight here. I imagine she wandered from the trail into one of those we haven't checked. It will just be a matter of time until we can get them all. But we've got to get you out of here first."

He thought she was going to protest. He was surprised. The childish April was gone forever.

"I want to go with you — but I'd only be in the way. I don't have the strength to make it." Tears streamed down her face. "Oh, Jason, Sancho, Dr. McBain — find her, please!"

"We'll find her." Matt's promise was a vow, but Sancho had other things on his mind. He had been watching the sky.

"The first thing we have to do is get you back to town and get more supplies. Jason, you can ride double. Take April home. Get another horse and more food."

April turned away to snatch her sweater, but she heard Sancho's low-voiced command. "Bring a medical kit, too. We don't know what we'll find."

April didn't show she had heard. The best way she could help Autumn was to get home, out of their way, although it would be

the hardest thing she'd ever done. But un-
nerved as she was from those days and
nights alone in a canyon with a dying man,
she would be no help on a search.

"Doc, we'll get them across that place in
the trail, then find something to cover up
Reed. The sheriff'll send out someone to
get him."

It was a grim task. Even though the man
had been warped, twisted, what an end for
him. What a waste of a life!

Quint Reed hadn't been any older than
Matt McBain. Now his life was over, gone,
thrown away because of a viciously planned
act. Sancho and Matt were silent as they finished their task and once more crossed the
treacherous spot in the trail.

"I'm glad to get across here," Sancho said.
"Whoever comes out for Reed will have to
do some trailwork. There's another storm
coming."

"How can you tell?" The sky was clear,
blue, only a few white clouds in the distance.

But Sancho only grinned. "I don't know. I
just can. Why we had to have two storms
when we usually don't get one all summer I'll
never know. Come on, let's go find Autumn!"

Sancho had been right. As usual, Matt

thought, huddled under his tarp near a dying fire. Actually, it was a drowning fire. The rain had fallen in torrents. When it finally stopped, everything was soaked. Never had the doctor spent a more miserable night. Yet it wasn't just the rain. That he could have handled. It was the thought of Autumn out in that storm somewhere that hurt him. Unprotected, surely without food by now. Could she make it? He cheered himself thinking of her superb health. Yet she had grown thin over the winter, worrying about April. Would she be able to stand the elements this night?

Sancho answered his unspoken questions. "She's a canyon girl, Doc. Don't forget that." Something in his tone of voice helped more than his words. It was true. She might be off in a side canyon, lost even, but Autumn Dale would find shelter somehow.

Shivering in his tarp, Matt McBain felt his head grow heavy, fall to his chest, and he slept.

Chapter 15

If the search party had only known how close they were to Autumn they would have gone into one more side canyon before heading for the valley entrance near the end of the main trail. She had walked and walked, resting only when she had to, trying desperately to remember how the trail had looked in the darkness when she had first ridden it.

Things looked different in daylight and on foot. At first it had been easy. There was the steep canyon to one side. But when it came to a point where there were red-rock walls on both sides of the trail, then the side trails became confused with the main one.

It was into one of the side trails Autumn wandered. She hadn't realized on that dark and miserable night the main trail had taken a sharp turn. It was a side canyon trail which went straight ahead. In her effort to make it out she hesitated at the fork. It must be this one that led out.

My problem is that I don't know how it's *supposed* to look, she thought. Her weary feet stepped more and more slowly. Recent events had taken their toll. At least it was easier walking here. She could see some vegetation starting, just as it should have done. But hours later she wasn't so sure. Was it right? Or was this just an extremely large canyon? By nightfall she was totally confused.

The next day she retraced her steps, or did she? She had been so sure she was on the right trail that when she started back she was confronted with other branching trails she hadn't even noticed before. Then came another day or so. The last straw was when she saw again a weird red-rock formation in the form of a gargoyle. She had noticed it earlier because of its ugly leering. That had been hours before. Now here it was, its fiendish stare even uglier. She had been walking in a circle!

How long had it been since she left April? Once more night fell. She had almost lost track in the endless walking. It was — it couldn't be! But it was. Three nights had passed. Tomorrow would be the fourth day! What if Quint Reed had gotten better and tried to harm April? All sorts of horrible pictures began to form in Autumn's mind, alone in the side canyon. Maybe she shouldn't have left April, but what other choice had there been? They could have been trapped by another slide, sealed off into a canyon where no one could find them.

Autumn's weariness mercifully blotted out further thought. But when she woke up it was to sit bolt upright, frightened, clutching her blanket. What was that rustling in the scrub brush behind her? She had no weapon of any sort. Thank heavens it was starting to get light. She cautiously edged back from where she had been sleeping. A huge shape in the dim morning formed, then stepped out.

"King!" In a moment Autumn was hiding her face in the shaggy mane of her own wonderful horse, bursting into tears with her arms around his neck. A little prayer of thankfulness shot through her. Things would be all right now.

By the time the sun was high, Autumn had made her way back to the main trail, leaving most of the guidance to King. He had evidently seen the vegetation and taken the branch trail to eat. Now at her command, "Home, King!" his ears perked up.

When they reached the main trail Autumn hesitated. Should she go back for April? But if Quint were still alive, they could never get him across that slide area. Autumn wasn't even sure April could make it across. No, she had better go back to Dale, get help, and come back. There was regret, almost apology in her voice as she headed King back up the trail.

"I'm sorry, April. It has to be this way." A wave of weakness went through her. Lack of food had sapped her strength. Could she make it? She had to. April's life depended on her getting help. April wouldn't starve, but who was to say what mental anguish she would suffer, alone in that forsaken place with Quint Reed? Just a short time after the men reached the slide area, Autumn was headed back up the main trail, holding the reins by sheer will power. She never remembered most of the trail, only that King sometimes turned his head, nickering as if to encourage her. Somehow in the confusion she had lost her hat and the afternoon sun beat down.

I must hold on, I must hold on. Step, King. Left, right. Left, right. Home, King, home. She drooped in the saddle, too tired to even realize when they got back on the main road leading to Dale. She was a pathetic figure. Dusty, tear-stained, a woman who had experienced things almost beyond her limits of strength.

That was the way Mrs. Jimson first saw her. Ever since she had directed the search party down the trail, she had kept vigil, only sleeping a few hours at night. All day long she kept her door open to the sun so she could see when they came back. It was good, feeling she had been able to help.

Annie Wells had ridden over one day with little Faith, sharing her concern for the girls. When Mrs. Jimson had tried to apologize, Annie had spoken from the depths of her big heart.

"Don't you go worrying about that. We all go off the beam sometimes. You just be glad you're well now and we're so thankful you were here! If you hadn't been, none of us would have known anything about those girls! Seems as if you just must have been sent back at that exact time so's to be here when we needed you!"

How long it had been since anyone had needed Mrs. Jimson! In a faltering voice she managed to get out, "I wish you'd call me Ellen."

"Sure will." Annie stood, taking Faith. "Well, I've got to be getting home. But you come over when you can — Ellen."

Ellen Jimson thought of her words: "sent back . . . exact time . . . when we needed you." Then she noticed the girl reeling in the saddle just down the dusty road from her place. It was surprising how fast she could move, catching the horse's reins, leading him up to the cabin, and how tender were the arms that helped get Autumn down. The hot sun had done its work well. The girl was feverish, lips parched, almost incoherent.

"Got to help April . . . so tired." She collapsed on the bed, never knowing when Ellen removed the filthy clothing, bathed the girl's hands and blistered feet, forced water then broth between the clenched teeth. With all her heart Mrs. Jimson wished for a telephone, any kind of communication with someone else. There was no one near and she didn't dare leave Autumn. From the girl's delirious babbling she managed to piece together most of the story. But she was so busy most of the time she didn't have time for anything except caring for her unexpected patient, wishing someone would come.

Ellen Jimson couldn't know that during the storm of the same day Autumn came to her place, a drenched Jason Wells and April Dale rode past. For a moment Jason slowed, wondering if he should stop and ask Mrs. Jimson if she'd seen anyone. But only for a moment.

April was all in, she needed to get home. It was a tender Jason who kissed his girl good-bye at the door, turning her over to Letty's welcome arms, noticing Dr. Archer in the background. He explained only briefly, then despite the storm, pounded on the store-keeper's door and got fresh supplies. The horses were replaced by fresh ones. Maxine Phillips saw to that. In a surprisingly short time he was back on his way.

Again when he passed the Jimson place, he almost stopped. But the windows were dark. He couldn't know Ellen Jimson was even then sitting close by Autumn's bed, watching over her by a small candle. Light had seemed to bother the girl. Outside, Jason shrugged and went on. The storm had stopped. If he hurried, he knew exactly where he could find Dr. McBain and Sancho. They'd be ready to start searching in the morning.

For another three days the three men searched every canyon. In the last canyon, the big side canyon where Autumn had spent so many hours wandering aimlessly and in a circle, Sancho found what he sought.

"Footprints." He frowned. "Look, there are also hoof prints. Those are King's prints!"

Dr. McBain looked at him in surprise. "How can you be sure?"

Sancho's face split in a wide grin. "I helped shoe him for Autumn."

This put a whole new slant to things. If she had a horse, then that meant . . .

"She must already be home!" Jason's feelings came out in a whoop. "While we've been searching, she must be back in Dale."

Sancho shook his head in agreement. "These tracks are two or three days old, probably made the same day you took April home, Jason."

Jason frowned. "Then why didn't we overtake her? She wasn't home when we got there."

"I don't know." Sancho couldn't add any more. He swung back to the saddle. "This is the last canyon. Let's go back to town and see what happens." He didn't add that he felt defeated. If Autumn was not in Dale, then he wouldn't know what to do. He carefully kept his shoulders from slumping.

"She'll be there, you wait and see." His expert tracking eyes followed the path of the horse. Many times it had been washed out by the rain, but here and there was a trace of how King had stepped slower and slower, carrying the almost inert form on his back.

Sancho drew his brows together. Had Autumn been hurt, that she rode that way? It was all there to read in the tracks. Or was she just tired, worn out? It was all he could do to keep his thoughts to himself, but he had seen how Jason and especially Doc McBain looked. No need to worry them more . . . at least not yet.

When they neared Jimson's place, Sancho's heart beat faster. Those were King's tracks here and there, nearly obliterated by storm and Jason's tracks, but definitely leading up to the little cabin! He motioned Jason back.

"Doc, go check with Mrs. Jimson."

When Matt had gone, Sancho told Jason, "She's here, but I don't know what shape she's in." They weren't long in finding out.

Dr. McBain was in and out of the cabin in a flash. "Ride for all you're worth and get my car. Autumn's here but she's pretty sick. Sunstroke, exposure, worry — it's all played its part."

Jason was gone before Matt finished speaking. He burst into Big Rock Hospital, demanding Matt's keys. Dr. Archer and Letty were on duty, busy with a patient who sat right up from where he had been lying on the table waiting for stitches. The patient demanded if Autumn was okay.

"She's sick but she'll be all right." Before

they had finished their job, the car was back and Dr. McBain was carrying Autumn inside. Ellen Jimson was right behind them. Dr. McBain had told her on the way in, she had done just right. If she had left Autumn in her delirium, the girl might have gotten up and gone back out looking for April. It wasn't until Autumn was in bed and April had come in, that things settled down.

April took her sister's hand and said clearly, "I'm here, Autumn. *Everything is all right. Everything is fine.*"

The incoherent mumbling stopped and for the first time Autumn slept. There were traces of gray in Dr. McBain's face as they slipped out. Ellen Jimson had asked if she could stay with the girl. Dr. McBain looked at Letty. April needed her at home. And Maxine had already put in a twelve-hour shift.

"Yes. If there is any change whatsoever, call me. I'll be in the office."

Jason opened his mouth to protest, knowing how tired the doctor must be, but the emerald eyes bored into his, daring him to comment.

Jason snapped his lips shut and turned to April. "I'll take you and Letty home."

But Dr. Archer shook his head. "You may take April home. I'm taking Letty home. In

233

fact, as soon as Autumn is ready for it, I'm taking Letty home permanently. We've found in all this trouble we both need someone. From the looks of things" — he peered over his glasses at Matt — "I'll be losing my star boarder." His keen glance took in Jason. "Letty will be losing her charge now that April's going to be all right. Besides, I expect you can take pretty good care of her, Jason. So we're getting married. Don't think you young folks are the only ones around here who can care about each other!"

Leaving them all gaping, he and Letty marched out proudly.

Maxine and Sancho had already gone, then Jason and April. Only Dr. McBain had been left at the hospital. Fortunately for him, again there was only the one patient — Autumn.

He slipped into her room and nodded to Ellen. "I'll take over for a little while. You get some rest. I'll call you if I need you."

Their eyes met and both knew he would not be calling her. This was his night to keep vigil. Ellen smiled. She knew now what she would do with her life. In the dark, still hours of caring for Autumn she had wished passionately she knew more of what to do. Tomorrow, or the next day, or the next, she would ask Dr. McBain the best way to learn nursing, where to go, whether to try for an RN or simply become an LPN. She was only a little over forty. That meant many years of service to others — perhaps even in Dale, if they could use her.

Autumn seemed to be coming back from a far country. What was dripping on her hand? Rain? Was she still back in the canyons? But how could that be? She dimly remembered Mrs. Jimson helping her off the horse.

What seemed like months later April had said, "Everything's all right." She had known she could relax. Would she ever again be so afraid as she had been, wondering if she could make it?

She tried to move her hand out of the drops, but someone was holding it. Someone with a strong grip. With all her strength, Autumn opened her eyes. The deep sleep had done her good, more than anything else. It had been untroubled. Now she was tired, her body ached, but her mind felt clear, for the first time in days.

Wonderingly she looked around the hospital room, then at the bent head above her hand. For a moment she closed her eyes again. Joy so exquisite it seemed mixed with pain had filled her at the sight of that tousled, bent head, fiery red hair spread out against the white sheet of her bed. When she opened her eyes again, he was still there, the big doctor kneeling beside her bed.

In all the years ahead I may never see him like this again. Autumn knew it was an unguarded moment, her awakening to find him there. It was his tears, the tears of a strong man who had nearly lost his love, which had fallen on her hand. She felt the mist rise in her own eyes, a mist of gladness. *I won't even have to tell him, he'll understand.* There would be passionate moments, laughing moments, and with red hair on both sides, probably many moments of anger, quick, flashing, over as soon as they had begun. But of every moment they would share Autumn would never cherish one more than seeing him like this, the proud Dr. Matthew McBain kneeling beside her, giving thanks for her life and safety.

As if he could feel the intensity of her gaze, the red head lifted. The emerald green eyes softened by recent tears met hers unashamedly.

She reached out her arms. "I love you. I always have."

It was enough. Their kiss which started softly, tenderly, became a promise, a pledge of life to one another, as long as they both should live. 🌸

The employees of Thorndike Press hope you have enjoyed this Large Print book. All our Large Print titles are designed for easy reading, and all our books are made to last. Other Thorndike Press Large Print books are available at your library, through selected bookstores, or directly from us.

For information about titles, please call:

(800) 223-1244
(800) 223-6121

To share your comments, please write:

Publisher
Thorndike Press
P.O. Box 159
Thorndike, Maine 04986